1692

A fusillade of fire broke out

Reese heard the CIA man grunt as an AK round hit right below his ribs. A second round tore into the agent's left shoulder and spun him back over onto his back.

When Reese started to crawl over to him, Sylvan waved him off. "Get your people outta here!" he yelled, his faded blue eyes glazed with pain. "I'll cover you!"

"Santelli!" Reese shouted as he reached the wounded man. "Sylvan's down! Cover us!"

Snatching a grenade from the side of his ammo pouch, Santelli pulled the pin and threw it as far in front of him as he could. Under the cover of the explosion, he rolled to the left and popped up in a new firing position, his CAR blazing again.

A sudden powerful explosion slammed into Reese. Red-hot shrapnel sang through the air, and clumps of damp earth showered down all around him.

"Incoming!" he shouted as he rolled over to cover the wounded Sylvan with his own body.

D0324425

HATCHET

THE FRENCHMAN

Knox Gordon

A GOLD EAGLE BOOK FROM

WORLDWIDE®

TORONTO • NEW YORK • LONDON
AMSTERDAM • PARIS • SYDNEY • HAMBURG
STOCKHOLM • ATHENS • TOKYO • MILAN
MADRID • WARSAW • BUDAPEST • AUCKLAND

First edition October 1992

ISBN 0-373-63206-1

Special thanks and acknowledgment to
Michael Kasner for his contribution to this work.

THE FRENCHMAN

THE FRENCHMAN

Author's Foreword

Along with the North Vietnamese government in Hanoi and their Vietcong allies, there were many other people who worked to bring about the overthrow of the democratic government in South Vietnam. In doing so, they also wanted to see the United States of America take a fall it would require years to recover from.

Not all of the people providing aid and comfort to the enemy were Vietnamese, however. Some were Americans and many were from nations who were supposed to be aiding us in the fight against Communist aggression in Southeast Asia. Journalists, businessmen, bankers, merchants and politicians all lent a hand in the dirty business of betrayal, sabotage and clandestine support of the Communists.

From case to case, the motivation for betrayal differed. Some did it for love, others for money or because they believed that communism would create a "Workers' Paradise" in South Vietnam. For others, betrayal was an act of faith required by the liberal, anti-anything-American, "right thinking" of the day. Most of them, however, really did what they did for their own selfish motives and didn't give a damn about the eventual fate of the South Vietnamese people.

There was a Frenchman who was a top VC agent in South Vietnam. In fact, there were several Frenchmen who did everything they could to insure the fall of South Vietnam and the defeat of the United States. Many of them felt that since France had been forced out of Southeast Asia, they were not willing to see the area fall into the American sphere of influence. Others belonged to the large French Communist Party of the day.

Except for historical figures, the Frenchman in this novel, like all the other characters, is a work of fiction. But then, the Frenchman was always elusive.

1

August 12, 1968, Saigon

The streets of Saigon steamed under an overcast, early-afternoon sky. Though it had stopped raining, the air was thick with the monsoon, almost thick enough to drink. Now that the shower had passed, the street vendors came out from under their shelters, pulled the plastic sheeting off of their small stalls and got back to business.

Five American officers wearing clean jungle-fatigue uniforms worked their way in between the stalls along a side street just off Tu Do. Earlier that morning their fatigues had been crisply starched and ironed, but the humidity had long since erased the creases and soaked out the starch. It was sheer futility to starch fatigues during the monsoon season, but old habits die hard, even in Southeast Asia.

The five officers, all lieutenant colonels and majors with staff positions in MACV, turned into a small open-front restaurant nestled between two street vendors' stalls. The Chez Charles was not an impressive establishment, but it was one of the better French cafés in Saigon.

"*Bonjour,* Monsieur Charles," LTC Dan Simpton greeted the owner and head waiter.

Charles de Gaulle Farman bowed slightly. *"Bonjour mon Colonel,"* the half-French Vietnamese said. "Your usual table?"

"Yes, please. There's five of us."

"This way, please."

After taking the American's orders, the waiter quickly returned with a one-liter bottle of an Algerian rosé and poured the wine for them. Leaving the bottle on the table, Charles retreated to his position by the open front of the restaurant.

The American officers talked as they sipped their wine and waited for their lunch, but they restricted their conversation to strictly neutral topics such as the Saigon social scene, who was sleeping with whom and news of mutual acquaintances. Even though Charles Farman had been cleared by both American and South Vietnamese Intelligence, the officers knew better than to talk shop outside of the secure confines of their offices.

At the discrete ring of a small bell, Charles went back to the kitchen and returned with fresh bread, butter, bowls of onion soup and quickly served the Americans. The men were hungry and found that the onion soup was excellent, as good as any that could have been found in the City of Lights itself. The broth was savory, the onions still firm and the cheese chewy.

Two Vietnamese men in nondescript street clothes appeared at the rear door of the Chez Charles carrying a cast-off American Army duffel bag. After glancing around, the older man pulled a black cloth up over his nose and mouth. Taking a small semiautomatic pistol from his pants pocket, he slipped through the door into the restaurant's kitchen.

A moment later he reappeared and motioned for the second man to come in. The second man pulled up his face cloth and, hefting the duffel bag, slipped into the restaurant. Inside, the Vietnamese cook and his two helpers were huddled on the floor, their eyes wide with fear above mouths covered with tape. Their hands were not bound, but fear kept them as effectively immobile as if they had been tied up.

Ignoring their captives, the two Vietnamese quickly armed themselves from the duffel bag. The fragmentation grenades they put in their pockets were American, the M-26 "baseball" grenades. For a job like this, the VC assassins could not risk the high dud rate of Red Chinese explosives. The rifles they armed themselves with, however, were Chinese-made AK-47 assault rifles. The Chinese Communists might not have yet mastered the technology needed to make reliable grenade fuses, but they had small-arms manufacturing down cold. Locking magazines into place, they slowly pulled back the AK's charging handles to chamber rounds and moved the selector switches down to the full-automatic position.

When Charles saw the two masked VC step out from the kitchen, he did not even have time to shout a warning before they opened up on the Americans. He threw himself behind the solid oak bar at the edge of the dining room as the AKs blazed on full-automatic.

The five officers didn't even have a chance to try to dive for cover before their bodies were riddled with 7.62 mm rounds. One man died with his soupspoon in his mouth and a puzzled look on his face. Another toppled face first onto the table, breaking his wineglass and driving glass shards into his forehead. The other three slumped in their chairs and tumbled to the floor.

As soon as the bolts of their AKs locked to the rear on empty magazines, the two VC ducked back behind the kitchen door. Snatching the grenades from their pockets, they pulled the pins and tossed them back into the dining room. Four sharp explosions scattered the dishes and silverware, tore through the sturdy table and the bodies.

Though bleeding from a dozen frag and bullet wounds, Dan Simpton was still alive. Leaving a wet trail of blood, he painfully crawled toward the front of the restaurant.

Stepping into the room again, the older VC threw his AK up to his shoulder, carefully took aim and put a single bullet into the back of Simpton's head. The American's back arched with the impact of the round in his brain, and he slumped forward, a fountain of blood spurting from the hole in his head.

The sirens of the Military Police were already wailing in the distance when the two Vietnamese stepped back out into the alley behind the Chez Charles. They ripped off their face cloths and quickly disappeared into the crowd.

THE ATTACK at the Chez Charles set Saigon on its ear. With the post-Tet curfew still in place, things had been relatively calm in the capital city for many weeks. The fear that this attack was the harbinger of a new wave of terrorism left the streets suddenly devoid of American servicemen. The thousands of bar girls, shoeshine boys and street hustlers, who depended on the free-spending Americans for their livelihood, went on an involuntary vacation. The Chez Charles was boarded up.

In his spartan second-story office, CIA Agent Dick Clifford frowned as he read the Military Police CID report of the attack on the restaurant. He absent-mindedly reached for the cup on his desk and took a mouthful of the cold black coffee. He spit it back into the cup and turned the page of the report.

Clifford was a sharp-featured, tall, thin man with close-cropped black hair and dark eyes. He came from a privileged background, but he, too, had been influenced by President Kennedy's inaugural speech and eventually came to believe he could serve his country best by guarding her against communism. He wore civilian clothes, but the short-sleeved Hawaiian shirt, chino pants and desert boots were as much of a CIA uniform as the jungle fatigues the grunts wore. The aviator sunglasses clipped through the first buttonhole of the shirt and the gold Rolex watch on his wrist were just part of the Intelligence agency's uniform. He did not, however, have a standard-issue CIA poolside tan. His pale skin told of a life lived inside the dim corridors of the MACV-SOG building at the edge of the sprawling Tan Son Nhut Air Force Base on the northwestern edge of Saigon.

The acronym *MACV* stood for Military Assistance Command Vietnam and, to most people outside the organization, the initials *SOG* stood for Studies and Observations Group, a harmless data-gathering think tank. To those on the inside, however, *SOG* meant Special Operations Group, involved at the deepest clandestine level of the war in Southeast Asia.

SOG had been formed in January 1964 to oversee the clandestine military operations necessary to conduct the war. Unlike the widely publicized, "conventional" unconventional war fought in South Vietnam by the Special Forces units, SOG's activities were known only by those with a strict need to know. These wide-ranging missions included strategic reconnaissance, Intelligence gathering, raiding enemy home bases, POW rescue, rescuing downed pilots and aircrew, training and controlling North Vietnamese agents, forming resistance groups, kidnapping or assassinating key enemy personnel and sabotage missions. All of these operations were conducted outside the borders of South Vietnam. Burma, Cambodia, Laos, North Vietnam and the three southwestern provinces of Red China were where SOG's secret war was fought.

Although their operations were supervised by MACV, SOG personnel took their orders directly from the Special Assistant for Counterinsurgency and Special Activities of the Joint Chiefs of Staff at the Pentagon. SOG's operational people were drawn from the elite special-operations units of all of the services, but most of them were Army Special Forces assigned to the Special Operations Augmentation Unit of Fifth Group, U.S. Special Forces.

Along with the military personnel in SOG, a large number of CIA, DIA and other civilian agents worked within the organization. Clifford's primary assignment was to evaluate the Intelligence gathered by the SOG RTs—the recon teams—and the far-flung CIA field agent network. Most of the civilians were in headquarters jobs like Clifford's, while others worked in the operational planning for the missions or in the logistics of equipping and transporting these clandestine forces.

Being a CIA man in a military organization had its drawbacks, but it also presented some interesting challenges. Investigating the incident of the Chez Charles was proving to be one of them. On the surface the attack appeared to be just another random VC terrorist act, but one of the victims, the late LTC Dan Simpton, had been the SOG officer in charge of counter-Intelligence operations. The four other men who had died with him had also been involved in counter-Intelligence operations targeted against the VC infrastructure in South Vietnam.

It was obvious to Clifford that they were not dealing with a random hit. It had all the earmarks of a targeted kill, an assassination. But against whom? Which of the five men had been the primary target? Who had gotten close enough to something the VC wanted to remain hidden that the VC were willing to

mount this kind of operation to take him out? Even
more important, who had leaked the information to
the VC? This was what he had been ordered to find
out.

It was the kind of spy-versus-spy operation that
Clifford had always wanted to get involved with, what
he had thought the life of a CIA agent would be like.
And there was no shortage of VC spies in Saigon for
him to investigate. The real problem was where he
should start. Every government and military organization in the city, both American and Vietnamese, was
riddled with them. Counter-Intelligence operations ran
constantly, but as soon as one spy was uncovered, a
dozen more sprang up in his place.

The problem was that the South Vietnamese government and military, as well as Vietnamese society
itself, was full of malcontents with an ax to grind.
Some of them were Communists but many were not.
What they all had in common was a burning desire to
bring about the collapse of the nation so they could
remake it the way they wanted it to be.

Most Americans had no idea of the extent of factionalism within South Vietnam. Much of the con-
flict was religious—the Buddhists fought the
Catholics, who fought the Cao Dai, who fought them
both—but there was just as much factionalism among
other groups. Labor unions fought against government control, black marketers and criminal gangs
against the police, and draft dodgers fought to stay out
of the army. Members of these groups were usually

more than ready to help the Vietcong if they thought it would further their own interests.

The first thing Clifford would have to do would be to get the assignment books of all five dead men and find out what they had been working on recently. He hoped that would give him something solid to work on. If his hunch was right and the Vietcong had purposely hit them, it could only mean that someone was in deep kimchee.

He reached for the phone on his desk and dialed the first number on his list.

2

August 13, 1968, Nha Trang

Special Forces Captain Mike Reese whistled tune-
lessly to himself as he stepped outside the wooden
building that housed the S-1 office at Nha Trang. The
afternoon sky was still overcast, but the daily monsoon shower had passed and the sun would come back
out shortly to dry the puddles between the buildings of
the compound. The Special Forces operations base
was small for a major American headquarters, but it
housed the Fifth Group, U.S. Special Forces, headquarters, which oversaw all SF activities in Vietnam.

Since he was visiting headquarters, Reese was
wearing standard-issue OD jungle fatigues with full
color insignia instead of the unmarked tiger-suit camouflage uniforms he wore around the remote base
camp he called home. The clean but washed-out jungle fatigues fit his six-foot, athletic build as though
they had been tailored for him. The famous green beret of the U.S. Special Forces—with silver captain's
bars pinned over the Fifth Group red, yellow and
green beret flash—covered his close-cropped brown
hair. His light blue eyes quickly scanned his surroundings, hoping to spot a jeep heading out the main
gate of the compound.

Reese commanded Mike Force Company A-410, a mobile strike force unit based at Dak Sang, a mountaintop fighting camp on the Cambodian border in the Fourth Corps area of operations. A-410 was assigned to CCC—Command and Control Central—at Kontum, one of the three MACV-SOG special-operations commands, and was involved in SOG clandestine operations.

Everyone knew what the conventional military forces were doing in Southeast Asia: the Army and Marines beat the jungle looking for the North Vietnamese; the Air Force flew over and dropped bombs on them; and the Navy sailed up and down the coastline shelling them occasionally.

Most people even knew about the elite unconventional units operating in-country, the most renowned being the Army's Special Forces. The Green Berets had received a great deal of media attention for their efforts to turn the indigenous minority tribesmen of Vietnam into light infantry units who could fight the Vietcong and the North Vietnamese army with their own guerrilla warfare tactics. Known as the CIDG, Civilian Irregular Defense Group, this was one of the most successful military operations anywhere in Southeast Asia.

Less well known but even more effective, however, were the mobile strike force companies, the Mike Force. These were specially trained and equipped CIDG units formed from the Nung Chinese, Montagnard or Cambode ethnic populations of South Vietnam. Most of them were airborne qualified and they specialized in heliborne operations. The Mike Force was a ready reaction force able to go anywhere in-country at a moment's notice to reinforce a CIDG camp, exploit a ground contact or to act as a lightly armed but highly mobile attack force.

Almost no one, however, knew about the secret war being fought by the MACV-SOG CIDG units like Reese's A-410. This was the real war within the war, fought deep in enemy territory, far from the highly publicized helicopter war televised on the six-o'clock news. These operations were so deeply classified that the name *SOG* was thought to stand for Studies and Observations Group to confuse even those high-ranking American military officers who did not have a need to know what SOG really did for a living.

What MACV-SOG did was kill the enemy. Their unofficial motto was Death Is Our Business—And Business Has Been Good.

Probably the most important of these SOG missions were the cross-border reconnaissance and Intelligence-gathering operations in enemy territory, known as Operation Shining Brass. With the asinine political limitations that had been imposed upon the movements of the conventional American forces in Southeast Asia, normal military operations could not be conducted in the North Vietnamese sanctuaries in the supposedly neutral nations along South Vietnam's western border. But, if the United States Army could not take the war to the enemy, at minimum they had to know what the enemy was doing. This critical mission was given to the MACV-SOG RTs, the recon teams.

These Shining Brass out-country recon missions were dangerous beyond any normal use of the word. The RTs were usually made up of only four to six men, one or two American SF and the rest Nungs or Cambodes. The teams were armed and outfitted with foreign equipment, wearing camouflage or specially made black uniforms resembling those of the North Vietnamese, carrying NVA rucksacks and often even enemy weapons. Just about the only thing that could identify them as being an American unit were the small rolls of U.S. C-ration toilet paper they all carried.

A vast array of support backed up these RTs: choppers on standby to extract them if they stepped in it, Tac Air fighter bombers to keep the enemy's heads down while they got out and high-flying communications aircraft so they could stay in contact with their headquarters and report what they were seeing.

Part of the RTs' support team were the units known as the Hatchet Force. These were selected Mike Force units composed of five Americans and thirty CIDG who had the responsibility of handling the missions that were too big for a six-man recon team to undertake. They were also tasked with exploiting the information sent back by the RTs and, in the event that a recon team was cut off from all other help, they were to fight their way in and rescue them.

A Hatchet Force assignment was exciting, freewheeling and dangerous, and Reese loved it. His A-410 Mike Force Company was Hatchet Force.

Although Reese was assigned to MACV-SOG, his routine military affairs were taken care of by the Fifth Group Headquarters at Nha Trang. Not that the matter he had come to deal with on this occasion was routine, however. With the signature he had just put on the bottom of a petition for divorce, he had taken the first step to freeing himself from a marriage gone bad.

Still, it would not be the last he would hear of it. Reese knew that his soon-to-be ex-wife would be certain to have the last word, the way she always did. But at least the papers were in the mill, and by the time his tour was over the divorce would be final. That was why he was whistling as he walked to the main gate to try to flag down a ride into town. For the first time in months, he truly felt like a free man.

On the road in front of the base, Reese hailed a passing jeep and hitched a ride down to Beach Road in the city. The ride took him through the middle of Camp John F. McDermott, or CJFM, the sprawling four-hundred-acre Army logistical support and supply base south of the SF operations base. Reese was surprised to see how much the camp had grown since the last time he had seen it. He knew that the base had been named after the first American killed there, but now no one could tell by looking that the war had ever passed this way.

CJFM was a dramatic contrast to the Special Forces headquarters, which looked like what one expected of a Vietnam outpost. None of the buildings was painted, and they all had sandbags stacked halfway up the walls. The perimeter had well-built defensive positions, and the armed guards on duty looked alert and more than ready to defend their turf.

CJFM, however, was just as finished as many stateside Army posts. White-painted headquarters buildings, huge warehouses, maintenance shops with shiny tin roofs and rows of barracks buildings with wooden sidewalks between them crowded the flat expanse of sand. It looked as though a little piece of America had been transplanted to Vietnam.

As the jeep turned down onto Beach Road, the late-afternoon sun glinted off slow-breaking waves in a picture-postcard bay. Motorcycle pedicabs putt-putted down a broad boulevard lined with palm trees, modern hotels and stately French colonial villas. Sea gulls slowly circled over the gleaming white sands of a world-class beach. Though he had been to Nha Trang many times, Reese still marveled at the tropical beauty of the coastal town.

Nha Trang was the third-largest city in Vietnam and had once been known as the "Jewel of the South China Sea". The French had turned the town into a world-class seaside resort and, even with the destruction it had suffered in the abortive Tet Offensive earlier that year, it was still one of the most beautiful spots in all of Southeast Asia. Although he knew he would quickly tire of the boredom of a rear area, Reese couldn't help but envy the men who pulled their tour of duty in Nha Trang.

Reese had the jeep driver drop him off by the King Tuy Tan Hotel on Beach Road. From there it was a short walk to the La Frigatte restaurant, where he was to meet his CCC operations officer, Major Jan Snow, for dinner. La Frigatte was a classic holdover from the old days of french colonial rule and still had a Michelin rating. After having learned what good food was all about during his earlier tour with the Tenth Group in Bad Tölz, Germany, Reese made a point of eating there every chance he could get.

Reese went to the bar to wait for the Hungarian-born operations officer. Jan Snow was Reese's superior at CCC, but with the informal camaraderie of the Special Forces, rank and position didn't matter as much as did the brotherhood of the elite. Reese was well into his second beer when Major Snow walked into the bar. Spotting Reese, he walked over to join him.

"Chivas on the rocks," he told the bartender without even bothering to greet Reese.

"I thought you Hungarians only drank fermented mare's milk or something like that?"

Snow made a face. "Koumiss," he said. "Nobody drinks that stuff anymore. Besides, today calls for something stronger."

The Hungarian drained half of the glass at one shot, took a deep breath and finished off the rest. He immediately signaled the bartender for another one.

Reese grinned. "Before you get too far in the bag, you want to get some dinner?"

"I could use something to wash the bad taste out of my mouth," Snow answered cryptically.

Reese didn't bother to ask Snow what had left him with a bad taste in his mouth as the waiter led them to a table out on the patio. If it was anything that concerned him, the major would get around to mentioning it sooner or later. Also, Reese wasn't in the market for bad news today. Signing the divorce papers had put him in too good a mood, and all he wanted was to enjoy his meal and a few drinks afterward.

"What are you going to have?" Snow looked up from his handwritten menu.

"I think I'll have lobster," Reese answered.

Snow put his menu down and signaled the waiter. "And I will have the Da Lat steak."

"That's horse meat, isn't it?"

Snow grinned. "My people have been eating horses for over a thousand years. We say that it puts lead in your pencil, as you put it."

Reese shook his head. "My people ride horses, not eat 'em."

"What do you do with your horses when they are too old to ride?"

"We bury 'em."

The Hungarian shrugged. "What a waste of good meat."

Reese laughed.

The waiter brought a loaf of freshly baked bread when he came to take their order. One of the best legacies of the French rule in Vietnam was the bread they had left behind. The hot bread was as good as any that could be found in the bakeries of *La Belle France*. The Algerian rosé wine that soon followed wasn't bad, either. It was young and a bit rough, but still a welcome change from half-warm beer.

Reese was buttering a piece of bread when the loud pop-popping of a 50 cc Honda motorbike with a bad muffler intruded on the quiet of the street bordering the restaurant patio. He looked up in time to see the bike screech to a halt and two young Vietnamese men pile off it. One of them clutched a square olive canvas-covered object to his chest and he pulled at a string on the front as he ran for the decorative stone wall of the patio. The string popped as it came out of the canvas, and a thin puff of dirty white smoke appeared. A satchel charge!

Shouting a warning, Reese cleared the Browning Hi-Power 9 mm pistol from his shoulder holster without his even having to think. Flicking off the safety with his thumb, he took a two-handed stance and fired. As he shot at the sapper, the second man raised an AK-47 and triggered off a short burst. Reese felt the rounds sing past him before the VC's weapon jammed.

Reese's first three shots stopped the Vietcong sapper in his tracks. The satchel charge fell from his hands to the sidewalk and exploded, blowing him to bloody shreds.

The second Vietcong dropped his jammed AK and took to his feet, but he wasn't fast enough to outrun Reese's Hi-Power. The next two 9 mm rounds cut him down before he got more than ten meters away. He stumbled and fell, then half rose as if to get to his feet and continue running. Reese's next two shots went into his back and put him flat on his face.

Seeing that the assailant was down for good, Reese spun around to check on Snow. The operations officer was lying on the floor next to his overturned chair, gasping for breath, his face gone pale. A small hole fringed with blood showed bright red against the olive drab of the right breast pocket of his jungle fatigues.

Dropping down to his side, Reese ripped Snow's fatigue jacket open and pressed the heel of his hand over the hole in his chest. The major was lung shot. His lungs would collapse and kill him if Reese didn't seal the hole.

"You're hit in the lung!" Reese said urgently. "Cough!"

Snow coughed weakly, a thin froth of blood coming to his lips. Even with the bullet hole sealed, if he didn't cough hard enough to expel the air that had entered his chest cavity, he would still die.

"Cough, damn it!"

The Hungarian coughed again, more strongly this time, and spit out a clot of dark blood.

"Can you breathe now?"

Snow nodded faintly.

"Don't try to talk," Reese cautioned. "It'll make it worse."

Keeping the wounded man upright, Reese dragged him back inside the restaurant where there was better cover. The explosion and gunfire had attracted the roving MP patrols to the restaurant, and the first jeep on the scene called for an ambulance. Reese kept his hand over the hole in Snow's chest until the medics arrived.

"I'll take over now, sir," a medic said as he knelt beside Snow and opened his aid bag. He quickly slapped a piece of surgical tape over the entry wound and applied a pressure bandage over it to control the bleeding. His partner readied a bag of Ringer's lactate, blood expander, and inserted the IV needle in the major's arm while the ambulance driver laid a stretcher beside him.

"We've got oxygen in the meat wagon, sir," the first medic reassured Reese as they moved the wounded officer onto the stretcher. "And we can keep him going till we can get him into OR."

Hearing the medic mention the operation room, Reese realized that they would have to put Snow under anesthesia to operate on him. As an SOG operations officer, the major knew too much to have uncleared personnel listening to him babble. Reese didn't want to delay his getting prompt medical attention, but at least he had to be there as a witness in case Snow let classified information slip.

"I'm coming with you," he said, grabbing the handles of his end of the litter.

3

August 14, MACV-SOG Headquarters, Tan Son Nhut

"You ever heard of a guy called the Frenchman?"
Dick Clifford asked Mike Reese the next morning.

The Special Forces officer shook his head. "Can't
say that I have."

After Reese had gotten Jan Snow to the Eighth Field
Hospital in Nha Trang the evening before, he had
placed an emergency call back to Kontum to let LTC
Newman, the CCC commanding officer, know that
his S-3 officer had been wounded. Later that night,
after seeing Snow through the operation to close the
hole in his chest, he had taken a room for the night in
the SF transient-officer barracks. He had just gotten
to sleep when he'd been awakened to take a phone call
in the commo center. The caller had been Clifford,
who'd said that he had heard from CCC about the
major's being wounded. He'd ordered Reese to get on
the morning ash-and-trash run to Tan Son Nhut and
report to his office as soon as possible.

Reese had worked with Clifford on SOG operations before, and a call from the MACV-SOG CIA
spook could only mean that he had another nasty assignment for him. The only question was, how nasty
was it going to be this time?

"As his name implies," Clifford continued, "the Frenchman is a holdover from the good old days. While we don't know exactly who he is, we do know he's been a big player since the French left in '54 and that he plays for the opposition. On top of that, his name keeps coming up in the black market business. He does guns, gold and drugs, and we think he's even involved with the white-slave trade.

"He may be a French Communist idealist, but we think that he's smarter than that. We think he's working with the Vietcong because it's easier to work with the little bastards than it is to fight them. In return for his being left alone to conduct business as usual, he runs an agent network for the VC and takes care of certain little chores like killing people."

"He sounds like a real sweetheart," Reese said. "But what's the connection with me?"

Clifford slid the CID report of the assassination at the Chez Charles across the desk. "Read this."

Reese quickly scanned the report of the attack and noted the similarity between that incident and the attack on himself and Jan Snow in Nha Trang. The use of both AKs and explosives was not the way the VC usually worked. Normally they used either one or the other, not both.

"You think the attempt on Snow and me was somehow connected with this?"

Clifford leaned back in his chair. "Yes, I do. Major Snow was working on a high-level SOG committee that has been evaluating our file on the Frenchman. The powers that be have enjoyed about all of him that they can stand and they want us to put that guy out of operation permanently. We've been closing in on him lately, and we think both attacks were an attempt to shut down the operation. I can't allow that to happen and I want you to help me.''

Reese frowned. "But how do I fit into all of this? This sounds like Company work, not sneaky-pete, run-through-the-jungle, Green Beret stuff.''

"I need someone to take up the trail again and ace this bastard for us.''

"But why me?''

"If what I think is true," Clifford replied, "I need an outsider to handle this, someone who's not known to the local VC people watchers. As far as anyone in Saigon knows, you're just another Green Beanie in town to get laid.''

Reese smiled. "Roger that.''

"You can go anywhere you want," Clifford continued, "and no one will think anything about it. And, to keep this even closer to our vests, I'm going to run this operation out of one of our safehouses in Cholon. I don't want you seen around here, either.''

"You think you've got a leak here in SOG?''

"It's possible. The access list for the Frenchman project is limited, very limited, and most of the names are connected with SOG. If the VC have learned what we're doing, there's a good chance that it came out of this building.''

"If that's the case," Reese said, "I'd like to bring Jack Santelli in on this. If I'm going to be operating like this, I'd like to have another man with me. Someone I know damned good and well that I can trust."

First Lieutenant Jack Santelli was Reese's XO back at his camp at Dak Sang, his second in command, and Clifford knew him from his previous operations with A-410. "No sweat," the CIA agent said. "I'll add his name to the access list and the directive."

Clifford handed Reese a filled-in form. "Here's your jeep chit. Just give it to the motor pool sergeant, and he'll fix you up with transportation. I'll call Santelli and get him up here on the ash-and-trash run tomorrow morning. When you find a place to stay tonight, call it in to the duty officer here in case I need to reach you.

"One last thing," Clifford added. "While you're in town, I want you to be armed at all times. Did you bring anything with you?"

Reese tapped his empty shoulder holster, "Only my Hi-Power." As did all visitors to the SOG building, Reese had left his pistol with the guards at the door.

Clifford pushed his chair back. "Come down to the arms room with me. I want you to check out something with a little more firepower."

In the basement-level SOG arms room, Reese was faced with a bewildering array of firearms. The place was well stocked with every conceivable weapon from silenced .22-caliber Ruger pistols to heavy-caliber, bolt-action, scoped hunting rifles.

"You guys wouldn't happen to have something simple like a Swedish K handy, would you?" Reese asked after looking at the array of weapons.

The armorer opened a wall locker, pulled out a Karl Gustav M-45 9 mm submachine gun and handed it over. Reese snapped the folding wire stock out to the extended position and pulled back on the charging handle to open the bolt. After inspecting the breech, he gently squeezed the trigger to let the bolt go forward. "This'll do nicely."

"How many magazines do you want with that?" the armorer asked.

"Two should do it."

"Only two?" Clifford frowned as the armorer loaded 9 mm cartridges into two K magazines.

Reese smiled. "If I need any more than two 36-round magazines to fight off the shoeshine boys and bar girls downtown, I'm in deep shit."

"It's not them I'm worried about," Clifford said. "It's the guys they're working for that concern me."

"Trust me," Reese said, patting the side of the K. "It'll be enough."

SINCE HE WAS going to be in Saigon by himself for the next several nights, the first thing Reese did was put a call in to the Saigon office of United Press International.

"UPI, Laura Winthrop," a throaty but very feminine voice answered.

"Good afternoon, Miss Winthrop," he said formally. "This is Captain Mike Reese, United States Special Forces."

"Mike!" she almost squealed. "Where are you?"

A broad smile quickly formed on his face. "I'm at Tan Son Nhut. How'd you like to have a roommate for the evening?"

"What are you doing in town? I thought you said that you were busy?"

"Something came up...I'll tell you about it over dinner."

"Where do you want to eat?"

"Can we grab a bite at your place?" he asked. "I've had about all of the restaurants I can take for a while."

"Sure," she said. "I'll get something on the way home."

"I've got a jeep, so I can pick you up if you can give me directions to your office."

He jotted down notes as she quickly outlined the fastest, but not necessarily the most direct, route through the maze of streets of South Vietnam's capital city. With the great influx of refugees since the Tet Offensive, Saigon traffic was the worst it had ever been, and it had always been a Chinese fire drill run amok. "Great," he said. "I'll be there in half an hour."

Laura laughed. "I'd better not expect you for an hour, then—you don't know the traffic this time of day."

"I'll see you when I get there, then. *Ciao*."

At the motor pool Reese located the jeep, which bore plain MACV motor pool bumper markings. As with everything else, SOG did not advertise its existence by painting its name on vehicle bumpers the way other classified units so often did. He signed for the vehicle, pocketed the keys for the steering wheel, gas cap and spare-tire lock and drove out of the air base.

The trip through town to the UPI office was every bit as bad as Laura had promised. In Europe, Reese had driven in Paris traffic and had even survived driving the "Death Strip" autobahn between Frankfurt and Heidelberg, but he had never come across anything as bad as this in his life.

Since the city was French in origin, Saigon traffic had always been chaotic, but what he was experiencing was unprecedented. It was downright ridiculous. At one point he found himself on a two-lane highway carrying four lanes of traffic going in three different directions. It didn't seem to bother the Vietnamese drivers in the least. Alternately using full throttle on their gas pedals and full blast on their tinny horns, they wove their way through the mess as though they were on an open road.

Reese had to pay such close attention to just surviving in the traffic that he didn't have time to sightsee, not that he would have wanted to see what Saigon had become since the Tet Offensive. Not only did Saigon still bear scars from the fighting back in February, but it was even more crowded and dirtier than it had ever been.

Back in the days of French colonial rule, Saigon had been a charming European-style city of some one and a half million people. Now its population had swollen to close to four million. Villagers fleeing from Communist activity in the countryside had turned the capital city into one massive slum from one end to the other. And even the slums showed the destruction that had been wrought when the allied forces had driven the North Vietnamese Army and the Vietcong out of their hiding places during the Tet Offensive.

Tet had been a sound defeat for the Communist forces, but Saigon's refugees had also been dealt a severe blow. They had tried to escape the war in the countryside, but it had followed them to the city and hundreds of them had died in the fighting. Thousands more had been left without any place to call home beyond a cast-off American cardboard packing crate.

With the slums had come the smells of too many people living without plumbing. Those who lived in Saigon had long since become accustomed to the stench, but Reese spent most of his time in the relatively clean air of the jungle, and it took a while for his nose to shut down.

He finally found the UPI building, a modern glass-and-concrete structure stuffed in between two French colonial villas and looking very much out of place. After parking in a spot marked Reserved, he asked the first person he found behind a desk where he could find Laura Winthrop.

With his green beret, jungle fatigues and shoulder holster, Reese knew that he looked as out of place in a newspaper office as a nun in a whorehouse, and it made him smile to see the reporters ducking for cover as he walked past.

"Mike!" Laura greeted him from her cubicle at the end of the corridor.

"You're looking good," Reese said. "It looks like you've fully recovered from your little visit to Dak Sang."

The last time he had seen her, Laura had been dirty, unwashed, smoke stained and dead-ass tired as she flew out of the half-destroyed mountaintop border camp she had come to do a story on. Even then she had been beautiful, but now she was stunning. Reese had to resist the urge to gather a handful of her long blonde hair to feel the softness.

"You ready?" he asked.

She threw a cover over her typewriter and grabbed her purse. "Let's go."

It was easy enough to buy something to fix for dinner. Regardless of chronic food shortages in the countryside, the very best that Vietnam had to offer was always available in Saigon's street markets. In a few minutes a dozen tiger shrimp, a loaf of still-warm French bread, some snow peas and black mushrooms were wrapped in yesterday's newspaper and paid for with American MPC. Reese had offered to buy the food with Vietnamese piasters, and the old woman had almost spit at him. With the war-ravaged Vietnamese economy getting worse every day, the American military scrip was the locals' only hedge against runaway inflation.

Back in the jeep, Laura gave Reese directions to her new apartment. "I moved out of the press villa," she explained. "I got tired of fighting off drunken assholes all the time."

Laura's new place was another French villa converted to apartments and, after locking the jeep inside the walls, they quickly went inside. "Help yourself to a drink," she said as she headed straight for the kitchen. "I'm going to start dinner. I'm starved."

Reese sipped a brandy while he watched Laura cook. That had been another thing his soon-to-be ex-wife hadn't liked to do. There was something about watching a woman cook his dinner that he had missed. He held his domestic musings tightly in check, however. Until he was finally clear of Judy, he could not even allow himself to think about getting serious with another woman. He thought he was in love with Laura and he felt that she loved him in return. But for now it would just have to remain a wartime romance.

"That was good." Reese sighed contentedly after the meal. "I'll make a note to remember to eat here more often."

"You still haven't told me why you're in town," she said.

"I'm just taking care of a little business," he answered cryptically. "I'll be here at least a week, if not a little longer. You mind if I camp out here?"

"It's going to cost you," she said with a sly smile.

"I think I can afford it."

Laura put her drink on the coffee table, walked over and stood in front of him. "Come on, then, soldier," she said as her fingers toyed with the buttons of her blouse. "You and I have a little business to attend to in the back room."

Reese drained the last of his brandy with one gulp, placed the empty glass on the floor and stood. In every man's life there come those times when he has to bow to the inevitable. This was one of those times.

"Never let it be said that Mike Reese ever stood in the way of business," he said, his hands running through her hair hungrily.

4

August 15, Tan Son Nhut

Early the next morning Mike Reese was waiting in his jeep when the Huey Slick flared out and touched down on the Hotel Three helipad at the Tan Son Nhut Air Force Base.

The first man off the chopper was First Lieutenant Jack Santelli, A-410's executive officer and Reese's second in command. Santelli was a wiry, dark-haired man whose dark eyes and olive skin indicated his Italian ancestry. He wore his tailored jungle fatigues with authority, and his green beret was canted down, almost covering his right eye. He looked like a movie-star version of a Special Forces officer, but the well-used CAR-15 slung over his shoulder was all business.

"Good morning, *Dai Uy*," Santelli cheerfully sang out as he walked up to the jeep. Noting Reese's bloodshot eyes, he added, "We're up a little early, aren't we?"

Reese cracked a small smile but didn't rise to the bait. His late evening with Laura had been the high point of their brief relationship. Though he had made love to her several times before, he hadn't realized exactly how extraordinarily sensual she could be when she wanted to. It must have been the right time of the month or something, because she had come after him last night with the grace and hunger of a hunting tigress. His back bore the marks of her nails, and he was so drained that he couldn't have gotten it up for Brigitte Bardot and a spot promotion to full colonel.

"Hop in, Jack," he said. "We've got work to do."

Santelli dropped his B-4 bag in the back of the jeep and slung his CAR-15 around so he could hold it in his lap with the muzzle facing out. Slapping a loaded magazine into the magazine well of the weapon, he pulled back on the charging handle to chamber a round and flicked the selector switch over to safe. Regardless of the MACV regulations prohibiting loaded weapons in Saigon, there was no way that he was going to ride through the streets of the city without having a round up the spout.

Glancing over at him, Reese thought that in a way Jack Santelli was an oddity in Special Forces, an Italian kid straight off the block in the Bronx. Most SF men, both officers and NCOs, were from the rural areas of America, particularly from the old Confederate states of the Deep South. Not too many men from the big cities ever found their way into an organization that spent most of its time fighting in the jungles of Southeast Asia. But then, Santelli wasn't your average New Yorker, and he preferred field duty to staying back at the base camp and playing XO. In the past four months that Reese had commanded A-410, he had learned that he could depend on Santelli, and the two men had developed a tight friendship, as well as a good working relationship.

"Where're we going?" he asked as Reese pulled out of the main gate of the air base and headed toward the center of Saigon.

"Cholon."

"I know you didn't call me all the way down here so you'd have someone to drink with, so what's up?"

"Clifford has a little job he wants the two of us to take care of."

Santelli shook his head. "Not the fucking Company again. Those bastards are going to get us killed yet."

"You'll like this job." Reese grinned. "It's straight out of a James Bond movie."

"Oh, shit," Santelli said. "I knew I should have gone to the woods with Kowalski."

"HERE IT IS," Reese said, slowing the jeep. "Fifty-one-fifty Hong Bang Street. Clifford's safehouse."

"This isn't a safehouse," Santelli said, eyeing the building. "This is a fucking fortress."

The place was a small French colonial villa with a thick masonry wall surrounding it. The top of the wall had broken bottles set in mortar and a triple row of razor wire stretched over the glass. A machine-gun bunker was built on each of the four corners, and a small but well-armed force of Nungs guarded the compound.

Reese pulled up to the wrought-iron double gate and honked his horn. Two Nungs quickly appeared and one of them covered the two officers with his M-16 while the other one opened the gate. Reese drove through, and the gate was immediately shut and locked behind them.

Before they could get out of the jeep, an American in civilian clothes stepped out of the villa and walked over to them. While the Nung continued to cover them with his M-16, the civilian checked their ID cards, comparing them to a list. "Clear your weapons," he said, and Santelli dropped the magazine from his CAR.

"Follow me, please."

The civilian led them up to the front door. "Mr. Clifford's in the first room to the right," he said, opening the door for them.

Reese and Santelli entered the room when Clifford answered his knock. The CIA agent looked as though he hadn't slept since Reese had seen him on the previous day. His clothes were long past merely being rumpled, his eyes were red rimmed and he badly needed a shave. His desk was littered with paperwork and the ashtray was overflowing. He stood when Reese entered the room and grabbed the crusty coffee cup from his desk.

"We've got our first break in this thing," the CIA man said as he poured himself another cup of coffee. "One of our sources has reported that the Frenchman will be meeting with the leaders of the VC network in Tay Ninh Province at noon tomorrow. You two are going to infiltrate the meeting site and terminate him."

"All by our lonesome?" Reese asked.

Clifford shook his head. "No. I've put together a little team to go with you."

"Who are they?"

"One of them's a Ranger sniper from An Khe, and the other is one of my people."

"I hope they know what they're doing," Reese said firmly. "I'm not about to try something like this with a bunch of fucking amateurs."

Clifford smiled. "They're pros, all right. The sniper's one of the best in the business, and Wild Bill's got more time in the jungle than you've got in the mess hall."

"Let's go meet these pros of yours."

Clifford led the two Special Forces officers down into the basement of the villa, which had been converted into an arms room and briefing area. The first man Reese saw was dressed in issue jungle fatigues with a subdued First Air Cav, horse-blanket patch sewed on the right shoulder, but he wore his jet-black hair longer than regulation. With his dark eyes and bronze skin, Reese knew he had to be an American Indian.

"I'm Mike Reese," he said extending his hand. "A-410 based at Dak Sang."

The sniper shook Reese's hand. "Spec Four John Metcack, sir. Hotel Company, Seventy-fifth Rangers out of An Khe."

"Nice to meet you, Metcack," Reese said. "And as long as we're going to be working together on this, you can drop the 'sir.' Call me Reese."

The sniper smiled faintly. "The guys I work with all call me Chief."

"Okay, Chief," Reese smiled back. "And this is Jack Santelli, my XO."

Santelli and the sniper shook hands, and then they all looked a little expectantly at the man standing beside Chief. He was in his late thirties or early forties. Instead of the usual CIA costume of Hawaiian shirt and wash pants, he was dressed in a faded, unadorned set of jungle fatigues and well-worn nylontopped jungle boots. His short-cropped blond hair was almost white, his faded blue eyes were cold and his face expressionless as he stepped forward. "I'm Sylvan, the security man."

Sylvan pointedly did not offer his hand, so Reese did not make an issue of it. "I'm Mike Reese," he said. "Who do you work with?"

The faded blue eyes swept over Reese's face. "You don't need to know."

Reese looked over at Clifford. "I don't work with people when I don't know who they are, Dick," he said evenly.

There was a slight pause before Clifford replied, "He works for the Company. He's a fix-it man."

"What does that mean?"

Sylvan's eyes smiled. "It means that I take care of problems, personnel problems."

"You're a hit man, an assassin."

Sylvan's eyes lost their smile. "That's one way of putting it, yes."

Reese nodded. "I don't have any problems with that, just as long as I know who I'm working with."

He turned back to Clifford. "One last question, though, Dick, what's the chain of command on this thing?"

"You're the mission commander," the CIA man replied. "But Sylvan will pick the target and will give Metcack the final okay for the hit. He also can call mission closure at any time."

"That's fine with me."

Chief listened to the exchange between the two white men. He himself had met Sylvan just a few minutes before and, like Reese, had not quite known what to make of him. As a sniper, he had no problem with men who made their living killing people. He saw himself as a modern Indian warrior practicing his trade, and he also saw Green Berets like Reese as being warriors, too. Sylvan, however, lacked something he could not put a name to, and that bothered him. He wasn't a soldier and he wasn't a warrior—he just killed people.

John Metcack was a Siletz Indian from their reservation along a river that ran through the Coast Range of western Oregon. The Siletz were a peaceful people, loggers and fishermen, but Metcack's grandfather had been one of the last warriors of the feared Tututni tribe in northern California. The old man had only been a teenager when the Army had rounded him up at the turn of the century and sent him into exile in Oregon after he had been caught taking part in a cattle raid on a neighboring white rancher.

Metcack's father was a logger, as were many men of his tribe, and the young boy had been left in his grandfather's care when his father was away for months at a time at the logging camps. Under the old warrior's tutelage, young Metcack had first learned how to hunt illegal deer for the family's table. He had spent many cold, wet hours hiding in the mountains of Oregon's Coast Range, waiting for a target to appear. The old man would only give him one round of ammunition at a time for the family's old lever-action Winchester deer rifle, so if he missed his shot, they would go hungry. The young Indian quickly learned to shoot accurately. He had had no other choice.

When he came to manhood at fifteen, the old man initiated him into the old warrior tradition and taught him how to hunt men, as well as deer.

As soon as he was old enough, Metcack joined the Army and volunteered for duty in Vietnam. He had done so well in basic training that he had been sent on to Ranger school and he had been invited to become a sniper when he'd arrived in-country. The white men in his Ranger company all called him Chief, but he didn't resent the nickname. He was proud of it because he was proud of his heritage and of his ability to kill his nation's enemies. When it came to the silent stalk and the long-range kill, he *was* the Chief.

"Now that the introductions are complete," Clifford said, glancing at his watch, "I think it's time for you to go over the uniforms and equipment. You'll be leaving here in a little over an hour, and I still need to brief you."

Clifford had a pile of tiger-suit uniforms and field gear on a table at the back of the room with several cases of C-rations and ammunition boxes stacked on the floor beside it. Reese sorted through the pile of tiger suits until he found a shirt and pants his size. He was glad to see that the uniforms had been well laundered. It was uncomfortable to wear brand-new, unwashed clothing on a mission because the stiff cloth chafed the skin raw. With sweat irritating raw skin, a man could be easily distracted, and distractions had a way of getting people killed in the woods. The load-bearing equipment was also well used and limber.

"How about field glasses, compasses and stuff like that?" Reese asked.

Clifford pointed. "There. It's all in the foot locker against the wall."

After changing into the camouflage uniforms and putting their field gear together, the men broke open the ammunition supplies, loaded up their magazines and readied grenades. Since he had brought his own match-grade 7.62 mm ammunition for his M-14 NM sniper rifle, Chief used this time to go over his weapon and sniper scopes one last time.

With half an hour to go, Clifford passed out the maps and started the mission briefing. The meeting was scheduled to take place in a forest on the Cambodian border known as the Straight Edge Woods, several klicks to the southwest of Tay Ninh City. Reese's team was to infiltrate the woods, locate the deserted Vietcong camp where the meeting was to be held, kill the Frenchman and withdraw. If the mission went as planned, they would be back in less than twenty-four hours.

Reese listened to Clifford's optimistic briefing with a certain skepticism, however. He had worked for the CIA man before, and every time the simple-sounding missions he initiated turned out to be a hell of a lot less simple when they got on the ground.

"What are we facing here?" Reese asked as soon as he could. "How many Dinks are we talking about?"

"Our information is that the Frenchman will have a two-man escort and he'll be meeting with no more than five VC leaders."

"So you're talking about eight men all told."

"That's right."

"Are we sanctioned to take them all out?"

Clifford didn't have to think about that for even a moment. "No," he said. "One of the bad guys in the VC group is our bad guy."

Reese sighed to himself. That was always the problem with working for the Company; nothing was every simple and up-front. There were always wheels within wheels. As far as he was concerned, as long as they had the chance, they should kill them all and let God sort them out.

"As I said," Clifford repeated, "Sylvan is to pick the target and okay the hit."

"What if Sylvan doesn't make it to the ambush site?"

"Call for immediate pickup," Clifford said bluntly. "Sylvan must call the shot on this one. I can't have a wild hit."

"That's fine with me."

"Any more questions?" Clifford's eyes swept over all four men. There were none, and the CIA man looked up when he heard the sound of helicopter rotors above the villa roof. "Your ride's here."

5

August 15, Cholon

The chopper that had landed on the flat roof of the villa was a matt-OD-painted Hughes OH-6 Loach. The machine was completely devoid of markings, even a serial number. In other words, it was a typical CIA mission ship. Without having to look, Reese also knew that the chopper's data plate bearing its manufacturer serial number would also be missing. Traceable serial numbers were the last thing the CIA needed on any of their SOG mission equipment. The pilot was equally devoid of markings. His OD flight suit was bare, and Reese didn't have to frisk him to know that he was also carrying no identification of any kind, not even as much as a matchbook from the Brinks Hotel officer's mess. This was a hundred percent spook mission.

Clifford accompanied the team to the roof to see them off. After taking Sylvan aside to speak privately, he turned back to Reese. "Good luck," he said.

"Right."

Crouching over to clear the spinning rotors, Reese took the right-hand seat beside the pilot while the other three men jammed themselves into the rear jump seat. When Clifford gave him a thumbs-up, the Company pilot pulled pitch to the main rotor with his collective control, and the Loach rose off the roof. Doing a pedal turn, he aimed the machine north and climbed for altitude over the city.

No one talked on the flight to the LZ. Even though Reese had put on a flight helmet and plugged in the intercom cord, the pilot had nothing to say to him. He had his orders to drop them off, and he knew how to get them there. The only thing Reese expected to hear from him on this mission was the request to pop smoke when he came back in to pick them up.

Several klicks out from the LZ, the Loach pilot dropped down to water-buffalo level and twisted the throttle all the way up against the stop. Reese had made these low-level, high-speed runs before, so he wasn't concerned. Nonetheless, he had to fight back the urge to pull his feet up each time they flashed over a rice dike and it looked as though the skids were going to crash into it.

A short time later the pilot banked his machine over and pointed it straight ahead to a dark tree line beyond the empty rice fields. It was the Straight Edge Woods. Nudging back on the cyclic control to pull the ship's nose up, the pilot chopped his throttle and collective at the same time. The unmarked Loach flared out for a landing in an abandoned rice paddy on the eastern side of the forest.

No sooner had the skids touched down than the four men of Reese's team scrambled out and raced to take cover behind a broken rice dike. As soon as they were clear of his main rotor, the Loach pilot pulled pitch sharply, sending the small machine skimming across the ground, tail high. A quarter klick away he zoom climbed up into the air and set his course to the Army airfield at Tay Ninh City base camp, where he would wait for the completion of the mission.

As soon as the sound of the rotors had vanished in the stillness, Reese took his field glasses from his ruck and surveyed their surroundings. This area was a common battleground between infiltrating NVA coming down from Cambodia and the Twenty-fifth Infantry Division units based in Tay Ninh City, and the Vietnamese farmers had long since fled to safer territory. When he did not see anyone lurking in the brush, Reese stood up and, motioning for the team to follow him, set out for the woods two hundred meters in front of them.

The first thing they had to do was to get into the woods and under cover. Because of the high level of secrecy surrounding this mission, the American units in the area had not been notified that they would be operating in their backyard. The last thing they needed right now was to have one of the Twenty-fifth Infantry Division's infantry battalions spot them and bring smoke down on their asses.

For the same reasons of security, Reese didn't have artillery or air support to call upon if they ran into the North Vietnamese, either. The only thing he could do if they got in trouble was to call the Loach back to extract them, and even that would be dicey. There were no chopper gunships they could call on to suppress enemy fire at the PZ, so they would have to have a stone-cold PZ before their ride home would come in to pick them up. The only way they were going to get out of this mission alive was if everything went as planned. There was no margin for error; even a minor screw up would get them all killed.

It was not the way Reese liked to conduct business, but he had no choice this time. The Company did things their own way, and when you played with them you played by their rules. He did, however, make a mental note not to let himself get talked into another one of Clifford's schemes if there was any way he could keep from it.

Once under the cover of the trees, the four men formed up into a patrol formation with Reese at the point, Chief taking up the rear in the drag position, Santelli with the radio at slack and Sylvan following Santelli. The Straight Edge Woods wasn't triple-canopy jungle, but it was thick, too thick for rapid movement. Since they didn't want to leave a trail for the enemy to find, Reese didn't chop a clear path through the underbrush. Instead, he moved down the animal trails and naturally clear areas, the same paths the Vietcong would use when they came for the meeting.

As he led the patrol, Reese kept a sharp eye out for booby trap markers along the trails. Even though the Straight Edge hadn't been the scene of any recent fighting, there was still the danger of booby traps that had been laid for earlier battles and then forgotten.

Reese finally called a halt as darkness fell over the forest. This area of Vietnam was as flat as a pool table so there was no high ground where they could safely hole up and keep an eye on the jungle below. He did find, however, a small rise in the ground with fairly good fields of fire to use for their NDP—Night Defensive Position. They quickly moved into the brush and dropped their rucksacks.

It was cold rations and cold mixed coffee for dinner that night. Sylvan sat away from the rest of them as he ate a rehydrated, freeze-dried Lurp ration and didn't even try to get in on the whispered conversation. Since their initial meeting back at the safehouse, the CIA hit man had not said more than a dozen words to the rest of the team. Reese didn't like having to deal with a "Lone Ranger" personality on a mission like this. It cut too deeply into the teamwork factor that was so vital if any of them were to survive.

With only four men, when the shit hit the fan, they would have to depend on each man doing his job and doing it well. Getting to know the strangers with you helped build confidence that you could depend on them. By now Reese had a pretty good feeling that he could count on Chief to do the right thing. But with Sylvan he was just going to have to take Clifford's word that the man knew what he was doing.

After stuffing their empty ration cans back into their rucks and securing their gear, the team settled down to wait out the night. Since there were so few of them, Reese had them bed down in a patrol star formation, a technique learned from the Israelis. A patrol star worked as well in the jungle as it did in the bare desert of the Golan Heights, where it had been born.

The four men lay on their bellies with their heads facing out in the form of an X and their feet close together in the center. One man would stay awake at all times, rotating the guard duty every hour. If the man on guard spotted anything, he would kick the foot of the man lying next to him, who would pass it on until they all were awakened.

Chief did have a PVS-2 Starlight scope in his ruck, and he brought it out so they could use it on guard. Though its usefulness was limited by the thick vegetation, the light-intensifying device would give them better night detection than unaided sight. With Santelli taking the first watch, Reese tried to sleep. From a few dozen meters away, a "Fuck-you" lizard sounded his mating cry over and over again.

Fuck you, too, Reese thought as he drifted off to sleep.

THE MORNING DAWNED cold and wet. It had rained most of the night, and even under the cover of the trees, the men were thoroughly soaked. On this kind of mission they hadn't brought ponchos, which would have helped to protect them from the wet. Wearing a poncho hindered one's hearing, and the rustle of the plasticized fabric could be heard by the enemy.

They ate cold rations for breakfast and then tried to work out the stiffness in their bodies from sleeping in the rain. Again Sylvan ate apart from the rest of them and had nothing to say. Reese would have loved to know what was going through his mind, but the blond hit man volunteered nothing and Reese knew better than to ask.

The plan called for them to move into a firing position five hundred meters from the clandestine meeting place several hours before the Frenchman was supposed to arrive. They would wait there until the target showed up, kill him and as many of his companions as Sylvan indicated before making their escape in the confusion. At least that was the way it had looked on paper in Saigon, but now that they were in the woods, Reese had some serious reservations.

He had never worked in this part of Vietnam before, and Clifford had assured him that the Straight Edge Woods did not present a significant terrain problem. Now that he was deep in the middle of the forest, however, he found that simply wasn't the case. He had learned yesterday that while the Straight Edge Woods might not have been triple canopy, it wasn't a city park either. The ground cover was dense. Not only would that make it difficult for them to reach their final objection, but it would also make it almost impossible to withdraw quickly after the hit.

Calling the team together, Reese brought out his map and went over the plan one last time. Since the going was a little rougher than he had planned, he decided to leave early so they would have plenty of time to prepare at the ambush site. There were no objections.

"Okay," he said in a whisper, "let's saddle up."

Reese took the point with Santelli as his slackman. Chief stayed in the center while Sylvan took up the drag position. Reese moved carefully as he made his way through the jungle. With a meeting of this importance, there was sure to be a sizeable VC security team covering the area, and he didn't want to run into them.

It was midmorning when the team arrived at the ambush site. Taking Chief with him, Reese went forward to recon the area. The meeting place was an abandoned VC camp in the heart of the Straight Edge. Reese's experienced eye told him that the camp had been abandoned for at least a year if not longer. The bamboo-leaf thatch roofs of the buildings were starting to rot, and the defensive trenches around the camp were melting back into the red earth under the relentless pounding of the monsoon rains.

The ground cover surrounding the camp had been cut back long ago when the site had still been an active VC base. But over the past several months much of the vegetation had grown back. Only the part of the ground that had been packed rock hard by countless Ho Chi Minh sandal-clad feet remained bare, but there were still good fields of fire for either an attacker or a defender.

"Where do you want to set up?" Reese whispered to Chief.

The Indian's dark eyes swept the surrounding jungle. With the Redfield ranging scope on his sniper rifle, he could hit a target up to a thousand meters away ten out of ten times, but this time it looked as though he was going to have to get much closer in. The dense undergrowth limited his maximum shot to just a little over three hundred meters. He pointed to a spot between two huge trees to the west of the camp.

Reese frowned. That put the deserted VC camp between them and their planned PZ, but it could not be helped. Chief was the expert, and it was the best place for him to make his shot. Reese gave the signal to pull back and, after rejoining the team, led them around to the trees Chief had picked.

The sniper had chosen his ambush site well. Not only did this position have a good field of fire for the rifle, but it also provided good cover and concealment for the other three men. The rest of the team quickly took up their security positions while the sniper prepared his firing site.

Even though the tiger suit he wore was perfect for jungle camouflage, Chief wished—and not for the first time—that he had one of those special sniper camouflage suits the Marines up in First Corps used. Made of rough burlap strips and netting, the Gullie suit made it almost impossible to spot a man until you were right on top of him. He didn't have a Gullie suit, but he had something that worked almost as well.

Opening his rucksack, he reached all the way down into the bottom and pulled out a thick wad of burlap strips ten centimeters wide and a meter long. The strips were dyed various shades of green, brown and gray. Selecting strips in the colors that most closely matched the vegetation they were in, he started tying them in rows on his arms and legs.

The M-14 NM sniper rifle had been painted in dull shades of green and brown, but that was not sufficient camouflage for the Indian. He wrapped one of the strips around the barrel of his rifle and the large silencer and tied it off. Another strip went around the upper handguard and a third around the stock behind the trigger guard. When he was done, only the muzzle end of the silencer and the ranging sniper scope were exposed.

Lastly he put a thick mesh cloth over his head and tied it in place with another of the burlap strips. When he was done, the sniper looked like a pile of green-and-brown vegetation. Even up close it was difficult to see the outline of a man with a rifle in his hands.

Reaching into his right-hand ammo pouch, he brought out a 20-round magazine of match-grade 7.62 mm ammunition with 180-grain bullets. After checking the seating of the ammunition in the magazine, he removed the magazine that was in the rifle and replaced it with the match-grade ammunition and pulled back on the charging handle to chamber the first round. He carefully lowered himself into position, lay down behind the rifle and arranged the loose ends of his burlap strips to further break up his outline.

John Metcack was ready to go to work.

Once Chief was in position, Sylvan joined him as his spotter. Not wanting to leave a boot print or a broken branch that could give them away, Reese didn't go forward of their position to look back to see how well camouflaged they actually were. He just took up his security position on Sylvan's left side while Santelli found a place to Chief's right.

Opening one of his ammo pouches, Reese took out a second magazine for his Swedish K and placed it within easy reach. He also took out two baseball grenades and, after straightening the ends of the pins so they would pull free easily, laid them in front of him.

Now they settled back for the hardest part of the mission, the long wait.

6

August 16, Straight Edge Woods

As he lay in the brush, Reese couldn't keep from glancing down at his watch every few minutes. Clifford's VC informant had reported that the meeting was to take place at noon, and the Special Forces officer hoped to hell that the agent's information was correct for once. He would rather fight all day than have to wait to fight for even half an hour. When he was in a firefight, at least he had a pretty good idea where the bad guys were and what was going on. When he was waiting, though, he could only guess.

Vectoring in on the scent of his warm-blooded body, clouds of almost invisible gnats swarmed around Reese's head. Even though he was out of the direct rays of the sun, the temperature quickly climbed as the morning went on. Sweat rolled down his face, streaking the camouflage grease paint, but he could not wipe it away for fear of wiping the paint off with it. He was also thirsty and itched all over, but these were minor discomforts compared to the agony of waiting for the unknown.

When eleven-forty-five arrived and there was still no sign of the enemy, Reese really started to worry. If the meeting was to take place as scheduled, the VC point-men, the security team, should have arrived already to check out the area. Something had gone wrong, but there was nothing he could do but continue waiting.

An hour later there was still no sign of the VC, and Reese started to crawl over to Sylvan's position. He didn't get far, though. A sudden fusillade broke out from the other side of the deserted camp, and the jungle turned into green hell as AK-47s on full-auto fire and RPD machine guns sent a hail of bullets in his direction. The tables had been turned. Someone had spotted his movement, and they were the ones who were being ambushed!

In his well-camouflaged position a few meters away, Chief hadn't been spotted. When the VC burst out from their cover and assaulted Reese's position, the sniper went into action. Taking the time to draw a careful bead before each shot, he calmly ran through the 20-round magazine in his M-14 NM. The muffled sound of the silenced rifle was completely lost in the roar of the firefight.

At least half a dozen of the black-uniformed figures went down and several more suffered arm and leg wounds. It was good shooting, but the problem was that it hadn't even slowed them down. For every man he put down, three more black-clad figures appeared.

When the rifle's bolt locked to the rear on an empty magazine, the sniper hit the mag release, slammed a fresh magazine in place, released the bolt and flicked his selector switch over to full-automatic fire. The first burst of full auto would blow the end plate out of the silencer, but right now he needed raw firepower far more than he needed silent kills.

The sniper rifle sputtered for the first couple of shots and then roared as the end of the silencer blew out from the increased gas pressure of fully automatic fire. The Vietcons faded back in the face of the storm of heavy-caliber rounds. Even keeping his bursts short, however, he quickly burned through the twenty rounds in the magazine. When he rolled behind the tree to reload again, the VC recovered. A storm of return fire shredded the foliage around him and sent splinters of wood stabbing into his face.

Reese and Sylvan were both burning through their submachine gun magazines as fast as they could when Reese heard the CIA man grunt as an AK round hit right below his ribs. A second round tore into the agent's left shoulder and spun him over onto his back.

When Reese started to crawl over to him, Sylvan waved him off. "Get your people outta here!" he yelled, his faded blue eyes glazed with pain. "I'll cover you!"

"Santelli!" Reese shouted as he reached the wounded man. "Sylvan's down! Cover us!"

Santelli's CAR-15 was smoking. He had already run through three magazines and was slapping the fourth one into place when Reese yelled that Sylvan was hit. Snatching a grenade from the side of his ammo pouch, he pulled the pin and threw it as far in front of him as he could. Under the cover of the explosion, he rolled to the left and popped up in a new firing position, his CAR blazing again.

A sudden, powerful explosion slammed into Reese. Red-hot shrapnel sang through the air, and clumps of damp earth showered down all around him.

"Incoming!" he shouted as he rolled over to cover the wounded Sylvan with his own body.

The second explosion was closer, and a searing blow lanced into Reese's lower ribs on his left side, sending a red-hot dagger of pain stabbing through him. He didn't have to look down to know that he had been hit. A third mortar round hit, but the singing frag passed over his head and shredded the underbrush.

"I told you to get the fuck outta here!" Sylvan snapped as he reached for his fallen weapon. "Go!"

Reese ignored the Company man and sent a long burst into the enemy positions. Unless they could get the mortar fire shut down, there was no way they could pull back. A fourth mortar explosion sent him back down on his face again.

Peering through his scope, Chief spotted a black-clothed figure kneeling behind a tree speaking into a radio handset. From the way the VC was watching the ambush killing zone, he had to be the mortar team's forward observer, the man directing the deadly fire. The sniper quickly zeroed in on him and triggered off a round. The bullet took the radio operator down, his body twisting as he crumpled over. Chief put two more shots into his radio backpack.

Now the mortar was neutralized. Without a forward observer calling the shots for them, the mortar crew couldn't fire because of the danger of hitting their own troops. With the mortar out of action, the

VC backed off to regroup and Santelli was able to reach the two wounded men.

Dropping down beside his commander, Santelli ripped open his fatigue jacket and examined the wound in his side. "It doesn't look too bad," he said. "But we've got to get you outta here ASAP."

"Check him," Reese said, motioning to Sylvan.

The CIA man's faded blue eyes were fixed in a dull stare. A jagged, still-smoking shard of steel was embedded in the middle of his back.

"Come on," Santelli said as he pulled Reese to his feet. "He's dead."

Seeing the other two men pull back, Chief increased his fire, sending round after round into any spot that could conceivably shelter the enemy. When the magazine ran out, he reloaded as he crawled backward out of his position during a lull in the fire. Crashing through the brush, he sped after the two Special Forces officers and caught up with them a hundred meters down the trail.

For the next several minutes the three men concentrated on putting distance between themselves and the enemy as fast as they could. When Reese stumbled and fell, they stopped to catch their breath.

"Keep on going," the sniper said calmly, spotting a perfect ambush point nearby. "I'll try to hold 'em up."

Supporting Reese with one arm, Santelli hurried him on down the trail. As soon as they were out of sight around a bend in the trail, Chief settled down in his new position and arranged his burlap camouflage strips around him. As he sighted in on the back trail, he really wished that he hadn't blown his silencer out at the VC camp. He had a perfect line of sight on the route the VC would use, but the minute he took them under fire, they would know exactly where he was. He snuggled down farther into his hiding place.

He didn't have to wait long before the enemy pointman appeared, moving fast but keeping a sharp eye out. Taking a deep breath, the sniper ranged his scope in on the man and slowly took up the slack on the trigger. The rifle spoke, and the target went over backward, the 7.62 mm bullet smashing into his chest.

Return fire started almost immediately, indicating that the main body had been close on the pointman's heels. AK rounds cut through the brush around the Indian, singing as they passed over his head. Ignoring the return fire, Chief calmly chose his next target, a VC who was a little too slow to seek cover, and put him down, too. Now, however, there was nothing to shoot at but their muzzle-flashes.

Peering through the Redfield scope, he detected a flash of movement in front of him slightly darker than the surrounding undergrowth. Sending a bullet after it, he was rewarded by a sharp cry of pain. The VC doubled their fire now, and Chief was forced to keep his head down. Knowing they were maneuvering against him, he decided that it was high time he unassed his position.

Scurrying backward, he ducked behind a tree and got to his feet. Flicking the selector switch back over to rock and roll, the sniper eased the barrel of the rifle around the side of the tree and sent half a magazine of 7.62 mm downrange. Spinning around, he raced down the trail after Santelli and Reese. Running flat out, he caught up with them five minutes later.

Now that Chief was back, the three men took off running down a trail heading to the southeast. Reese didn't have time to stop to read his map, but they were moving in the right general direction. As he ran, he reached for the handset to the radio on Santelli's back. "Black Dog, Black Dog," he radioed. "This is Bat Man, over."

Reese released the push-to-talk switch, but there was only the rushing sound of squelch coming in over the handset. Where the fuck was that Company Loach driver?

"Black Dog, Black Dog, this is Bat Man. Blue Star," he called again, using the SOG code word for an emergency. "I say again Blue Star. Over."

"Black Dog," the pilot answered curtly. "Send it."

"This is Bat Man, we are blown and on the run. Need immediate extract at Papa Zulu One, over."

There was a long pause before the pilot answered, "Roger, is the mission complete?"

Now it was Reese's turn to pause. What in the hell did the pilot mean by "complete"? They had been ambushed and were on the run, but he had no idea if the fabled Frenchman had even been with the ambushers. The real question, Reese sensed, was what did the pilot want to hear? It was not the best time in the world to get into a long discussion about the mission, so Reese told the pilot what he thought he wanted to hear.

"Bat Man, that's a roger," Reese radioed. "The mission is complete."

"Let me talk to Sylvan," the pilot requested.

Reese thought fast. "Sylvan's been hit. We need extract ASAP."

There was another long pause. "Roger, on the way."

"Bat Man, out."

As soon as the three men broke out of the woods, Reese stopped long enough to locate themselves accurately. Their scheduled pickup zone, Papa Zulu One, was half a klick to their right.

"We're almost there," he said, more to reassure himself than the others. The wound in his side still hurt, but it could wait. With Chief keeping an eye on their rear, they took off running again.

When they reached the PZ, the three men dropped down behind the rice dike facing the woods and fought to catch their breath. Reese reached for the radio handset again and keyed the mike. "Black Dog, Black Dog," he panted. "This is Bat Man, over."

"Black Dog," the pilot answered. "Go ahead."

Reese could tell from the sound of the pilot's voice that the transmission was being made from a chopper in flight, so at least he was on his way. "This is Bat Man. We are at Papa Zulu One and ready for pickup. Over."

"Roger," came the reply. "ETA zero-three."

"He's coming," Reese said as he handed the handset back to Santelli. "Get ready."

The men heard the high-pitched sound of the Loach's rotors before they saw it. Once more the Company pilot had the dull OD machine flat out, right down on the deck. Reese knew that a Loach could do almost two hundred klicks per hour at full throttle, and it looked like the CIA machine was topping even that.

In a flurry of dust, the small chopper flared out over the dry paddy and skidded to a halt several meters from the team. Reese jumped up and ran for the Loach.

"Where's Sylvan?" the pilot shouted over the sound of the chopper's rotors.

"He's dead!" Reese yelled back as he ran. "We had to leave him!"

The pilot was reaching for his collective to pull pitch when Reese reached the open door of the ship. As he swung himself up, the muzzle of his Swedish K slipped over the bottom of the passenger seat. Realizing that the pilot was trying to take off without them, he snapped the submachine gun up and jammed the muzzle into his ribs. "Hold it right there!" he yelled.

His face expressionless behind his helmet visor, the pilot took his hands off the controls. Holding the K on him, Reese waved Santelli and Chief forward. "Get on!"

The two men raced up and scrambled into the jump seat in the rear compartment. As soon as they were in, Reese swung in through the open door, dropped into the right-hand seat and, reaching for the shoulder harness, buckled it securely around him.

Black-clad figures were already breaking out of the tree line as the pilot pulled pitch and the ship leaped into the air at full throttle. Several of the VC fired their AKs at the small chopper, but keeping low to the ground, the pilot quickly sped out of range.

As soon as the Loach was clear, he climbed to a safe altitude and started to bank away to the north. Reese wasn't a pilot, but he knew how to read an aircraft compass and knew where Saigon was. Keeping his weapon aimed at the pilot, he slipped on the flight helmet so he could talk to him privately over the intercom.

"If you even think of taking us anywhere except straight back to Cholon," Reese cautioned, "I'm going to shoot your kneecaps out. I know enough about flying one of these things that I can put us down safely."

With a quick glance down at the submachine gun, the pilot shrugged and set course south for Saigon. No one spoke on the trip back.

The pilot flared out over the rooftop of the safehouse and chopped his throttle as the Loach touched her skids down. Reese unbuckled his shoulder harness and leaned over toward the pilot, the muzzle of his K carelessly aimed at the flyer. The pilot glanced down at the weapon and turned his head back to stare out of the canopy in front of him.

"I owe you one, mister," Reese said, his voice cold. "And if I ever run into you again, you'd better turn your young ass around and head the other way as fast as you can. You got that?''

The Company pilot nodded his head slightly as he continued to stare straight forward, his face expressionless. When Reese stepped down to the rooftop, the Loach driver was still looking out through his canopy.

7

August 16, Cholon

"We were set up!" Reese hissed. "They knew that we would be there. Someone in this fucking Company of yours leaked the fucking mission!"

Clifford sat numbly, staring at the jumble of paper on his desk as he rode out Reese's verbal storm. The CIA man had had words with Reese before but had never seen him this angry. The Special Forces captain was practically foaming at the mouth and jumping up and down. The problem was that Reese was one hundred percent correct. There had been a leak, and the most likely place was from within the ranks of SOG or the Company.

He had been afraid that something like this would happen, and that was why he had called in Sylvan and Chief to work the mission with Reese and Santelli. Like the two Special Forces officers, they were outsiders and they should have been unknown to the opposition. Sylvan had been brought in all the way from northern Thailand, and the sniper had never even been in Saigon before. It should have worked, but now Sylvan was dead. He had been a top asset, and someone would have to answer for his loss.

As the Great Bard said, something was rotten in Denmark and he could smell it all the way to Saigon.

"And just what in the fuck are you going to do about it?" Reese concluded.

Clifford looked up at him. "I don't fucking know."

That stopped Reese's tirade. He had never seen a time when the CIA man didn't have a plan. It might be a totally screwed-up plan, but he always had one.

"What do you think we should do?" Clifford asked with uncharacteristic humility.

Reese was momentarily taken aback, but he quickly recovered. "I think we should kill somebody," he snapped.

"Just who do you have in mind?"

"The sorry bastard who burned this mission."

"Where do you think we should start looking for him?"

"In the Central fucking Intelligence Agency."

Clifford got to his feet. "You're right. We're going to find someone in the CIA and waste him. First, though, don't you think that we really ought to make sure that we've got the right man before we kill him? I'd have to do too much paperwork if we zeroed the wrong guy."

Reese's eyes slitted. "Don't screw around with me, Dick," he said, his voice low. "I'm not in the mood for that kind of garbage right now. I almost got wasted out there today and I've kind of lost my sense of humor, if you know what I mean. There's something about walking into an ambush that'll do that to you every time."

"Are you finished?" Clifford asked.

Reese took a deep breath. "You're fucking right I'm finished. As soon as Santelli and I can get our stuff together, we're leaving. And the next time you want some dumb ass to play pop-up target for one of your missions, you can fucking well go yourself."

"So you're going to go back to Dak Sang and just forget about all this, right?"

"Something like that—" Reese stared him down "—yes."

"And you think that the Frenchman is just going to let you go on about your merry way killing Dinks and saving the world for democracy, right?"

"Why not?" Reese snapped. "I'm not a part of this James Bond bullshit of yours. I'm a soldier, not some spook. I'm going to go back to the border, mind my own business and leave you dickheads to play our dumb-ass spy games all by yourselves. As of right now, Santelli and I are out of this. We're gone, *Di Di Mau.*"

Clifford leaned forward, his eyes glittering. "Listen asshole, you're in deep shit right along with me whether you like it or not. As far as the Frenchman is concerned, you're in the same category as the late Colonel Dan Simpton and the almost-late Major Jan Snow. You obviously know too much about him and he can't afford to let you keep on breathing. You and Santelli can go back to the hills and play supersoldier all you like, but that's not going to save you. Sooner or later the Frenchman is going to track your young asses down and kill both of you."

"If he wants to fuck with us at Dak Sang, that's fine with me." Reese smiled thinly. "But he'd better bring his fucking lunch, 'cause it's going to be an all-day job."

"He won't do it at Dak Sang," Clifford said quietly. "He'll catch you the next time you go to Kontum. Or—" he paused to coldly smile "—the next time you stop in at La Frigatte in Nha Trang. Unless you want to hide in a bunker for the rest of your tour, you're going to have to deal with him now."

Reese hated to admit it, but Clifford had a point, a good point unfortunately. He felt his anger fade to be replaced by resignation.

"Shit," he muttered. "What do we do next?"

"Actually I don't know," Clifford admitted. "I think you'd better go clean up, have that wound checked out and get some rest. We'll meet here tomorrow morning and see what we have to work with. In the meantime I'll go over what I have and try to figure out some way to get another lead on this bastard."

"Just make sure it's better than this last one," Reese said, his hand automatically going to the field bandage on his side. "I've enjoyed just about all of this shit that I can stand."

"Before you go," Clifford said, rummaging around on his desktop. "I've got something for you."

"What's that?"

Clifford held out what looked like a set of orders and an ID card. "Your sanction papers."

Reese glanced at the card. It bore his ID card photo, name and social security number under the title Special Operations Card. The text under his name read that he was conducting unrestricted activities essential to the security of the United States. Persons with questions about his activities were instructed to call a phone number.

Reese smiled. "A Get Out Of Jail Free Card, right?"

Clifford didn't smile. "They're sometimes called that, yes," he said. "But it's not a joke. You'd better keep it on your person until this thing's completely over. It'll save you a lot of grief if anything goes wrong."

The infamous CIA ID card would not only do that, but it would give Reese immediate access to any facility in Vietnam, no questions asked, and would allow him to do damned near anything he wanted in the name of protecting national security. Even kill.

The other papers were the background data and the official sanction for the mission against the Frenchman, his license to kill, as it were.

"I don't have to remind you to keep those documents safeguarded," Clifford said. "And keep that card on your body at all times."

"Where's my cyanide capsule—" Reese smiled broadly "—and my invisible ink? Or aren't they standard Company issue anymore."

"Get the hell outta here," Clifford growled.

WHEN REESE SHOWED UP at Laura's apartment early that evening, he was wearing dirty, sweat-and-blood-stained camouflage fatigues, the uniform he called his tiger suit. He had a briefcase in one hand and a B-4 bag in the other, which clanked when he laid it on the floor.

"Mike! What happened to you?"

"Rough day at the office," he answered cryptically as he walked over to the cabinet and poured himself a tall glass of brandy.

She caught a flash of stark white bandage through the jagged bloodstained hole in his fatigue jacket. "You're hurt!"

He downed a third of the glass in a single gulp. "It's just a scratch," he said when he came up for air.

"What are you doing here? You said you were going to be out of town for a few days."

"I got back early."

His cryptic, curt answers jarred her reporter's instincts. He obviously didn't want to talk, but she just couldn't let it go. "Are you on some kind of SOG assignment?"

"Laura," he said firmly, refilling his glass, "I really can't talk about it, okay?"

"Okay." She smiled as her eyes flicked over to the briefcase on the table. "I'll bet you're hungry. I'll go down to the restaurant and get us something to eat. What would you like? Shrimp? Lobster?"

"Anything but water buffalo."

When she came back carrying a wicker basket filled with their dinner, she saw that Reese had showered, shaved and changed into a clean fatigue uniform. He said little, but kept his brandy glass full throughout dinner, and by the time it was finished, he had quite a buzz on.

Seeing that he was exhausted, Laura suggested that they go to bed early and he didn't argue. When she saw him wince as he sat down on the edge of the bed, she thought it would be best if they would not get too acrobatic. "Lie back, lover," she purred. "I'll do all the work."

When he lay back with that boyish grin she loved so much on his face, she let him feel the full length of her body against his. Then she straddled him and sinuously lowered herself down onto him.

Their lovemaking that night was slow and gentle.

WHEN REESE'S BREATHING told her that he was deep in brandy-soaked sleep, Laura carefully untangled herself and sat up in the rumpled bed. Slowly she swung her legs over the side, then stood. The night air felt cool on her sweaty skin as she walked over to the table where he had laid his briefcase. With a glance back to make sure he was still sleeping soundly, she picked it up and took it into the small kitchen.

She knew that she was taking a chance of completely destroying her relationship with Reese, but she hesitated only a second before opening the briefcase. She thought she loved Mike Reese, but she knew she loved her profession. Making a name for herself as a reporter, however, meant that she was going to have to hit on the big story. Both her journalistic and female instincts told her that her lover was involved in a big story, and she was willing to risk what she had with him to get it.

Laura had been full of youthful enthusiasm when she'd graduated from the journalism school at Colombia University and embarked on her career. She had understood that she was going to have to work harder than a man to make her mark in journalism, but she had not really reckoned with just how much harder it was going to be. Her first assignments in Vietnam had been to cover powder-puff pieces, stories with a woman's slant. She had accepted these assignments without grumbling because she knew that all rookie reporters had to pay their dues before they got the good assignments.

The problem was that after months of paying her dues covering refugee, orphanage and school stories, she was still being assigned women's pieces. Every time she asked her editor to cover a real war story, he put her off.

A month and a half ago, however, she had stumbled onto some shreds of information about MACV-SOG, the secretive organization that was conducting a secret war within the war in Vietnam. Laura had worked hard and followed her hunches about the lead until it had led her to Mike Reese's remote mountain-top Special Forces camp at Dak Sang. Her visit there had coincided with a massive NVA attack, and she'd found herself in danger of being killed but had gotten her story and it had been a good one.

Even that story, though, had not been the step up she had hoped it would be. In fact, it had blown up in her face and had almost gotten her thrown out of country. SOG had a long reach and they had used it to halt the publication of her story, sending her back to square one with a stern warning to keep her journalistic nose out of their classified operations.

She knew now that it had been a mistake to try to force the issue with SOG headquarters on her original story. When she had thought she was so smart and had forced their hand to let her cover the story, they had actually been biding their time, knowing that they had the power to prevent publication of anything she wrote.

This time, however, it would be different. Marshall, the old SOG colonel she had gone head-to-head with, was gone. The new man wouldn't know anything about her unless Marshall had put her on some sort of reporters blacklist. Also, this time SOG wouldn't know that she was working on a story about the shadowy organization. This time she had her own private source of information, and he was sleeping peacefully in the next room.

Her breath coming quickly, she took the document out into the light. The report bore red ink classification stamps on the top and bottom of each page, reading Top Secret—Noforn. The Top Secret marking was understandable, but what in the hell did Noforn mean?

Heart pounding, she quickly scanned the document. After reading through the pages twice, she put them down and stared blankly at the wall. If she had understood all the jargon and acronyms correctly, Reese was in Saigon to find someone called the Frenchman and assassinate him, pure and simple. "Terminate with extreme prejudice" was the exact way the orders were worded. Furthermore, to accomplish the mission, he was apparently working with men from a secret CIA operation code-named Project Phoenix.

She carefully put the papers back into the briefcase in the order she had taken them out, shut the lid and locked it again. Quietly she poured herself half a glass of brandy, knocked back a stiff shot and stared at the briefcase as the full implications of what she had just read sunk in.

A twinge of fear crossed her mind as she realized that she was sleeping with an assassin. She had just made love to a man who was going out tomorrow morning to cold-bloodedly track a man down and kill him. Though the night air was warm, she shivered and crossed her legs.

She knew that Reese had killed many men before. After all, he was a combat soldier in a war zone and a Green Beret officer on top of that. Killing was his profession, and he was obviously good at it because he was still alive. But this was different. If she understood the orders correctly, he was going to hunt a man down, a French national, and kill him in cold blood without even giving him a chance to defend himself. The orders specifically stated that he was not to try to capture him alive. He was simply to "terminate with extreme prejudice."

Since coming to Vietnam, she had heard dozens of euphemisms for killing and death; everyone used them to distance themselves from the realities of the war. Some of the words were meant to be funny and some were purposefully outrageous. But never had she heard anything as cold as "terminate with extreme prejudice." The phrase held about as much emotional content as the act of switching off a light.

After returning the briefcase to the table, she carefully got back into bed and eased up against Reese's sleeping body. This time, however, his warm bulk against her brought her no comfort. It was a long time before she drifted off to sleep.

8

August 17, Saigon

Laura was quiet over breakfast, very quiet. She hardly said a word as she and Reese sat and drank their coffee. Reese didn't spend too much time trying to find out what was wrong with her. His wound ached and he was more than a little hung over. He was also in a hurry to get to the safehouse to see if Dick Clifford had come up with anything new during the night.

"I'll see you tonight," he said as he picked up his briefcase and B-4 bag on the way to the door. "Maybe we can go out for dinner."

"That sounds nice," she said, and smiled weakly.

As soon as Reese was out of the door, Laura sat down and made notes on what she remembered from the documents she had read about the Frenchman the night before. She realized now that she should have taken notes while she'd had the documents in her hands. But she had been so shocked at what she was reading that the thought had not crossed her mind.

After writing down everything she could remember, she printed the words "terminate with extreme prejudice" and underlined them. That was the key to the story she had uncovered. Who the man was that was to be terminated was not half so important as the fact that his death had been coldly ordered by the American government.

Laura was young, but she was not a dope-smoking, antigovernment, knee-jerk liberal. She was aware that if the United States was going to win the Cold War, harsh measures were sometimes called for. Particularly in the shadowy world of espionage. And she had a hunch that this Frenchman was a spy for the North Vietnamese. Nothing she had read said that he was, but that was the only thing she could think of that would justify the termination order.

Since this wasn't something that she could research at the MACV press information office, she was going to have to develop her leads from her own sources. The problem was that she really didn't have any sources. Covering the women's stories in Saigon didn't put her in a position to rub shoulders with the movers and shakers in town. In fact, her best and only source had just walked out the door, and he didn't even know that he was the source.

What she needed to do was to talk to someone who knew their way around town. Someone who had good sources inside the various military and civilian agencies in Saigon. Someone who had been around long enough to have picked up rumors about a man known only as the Frenchman.

She smiled softly when the answer came to her. She had a perfect source to start her in the right direction, Simon Harrison, her one-time lover and mentor. Harrison was a British reporter who covered Saigon for the leftist newspapers in Europe, and she had run into him during her first week in-country. She had not set out to play the role of the damsel in distress with him, but the older Simon had picked up on her bewilderment at being on unfamiliar ground and had taken her under his wing.

He had also taken her into his bed at the first opportunity that presented itself, but she held no grudges on that account. Simon had merely taken advantage of her the same way most men would take advantage of an obviously lonely, willing woman. He had been there when she had desperately needed a friend, and it was not his fault if she had taken him up on his invitation to share his bed. He had always acted like a gentleman with her. Even when he told her that their brief affair had to come to an end, he had been gentle, and she still considered him a friend. She was also certain that she had a marker or two that were still good with him.

A quick phone call set up a late-morning meeting with her mentor and she hurried to dress.

WHEN REESE WALKED into Clifford's office, he saw that the CIA man was still wearing the same rumpled clothes he had worn the day before. There was a sour, unwashed smell in the room, and his desk was even more cluttered than it had been, only he now had two overflowing ashtrays on the desk. He looked like two pounds of shit in a one-pound bag, but there was a glitter in his eyes that hadn't been there the last time.

"I think I've got a lead on him," Clifford said.

"The Frenchman?"

The CIA man shook his head. "No. The asshole who's been passing information about the Frenchman Project."

"What do you mean?"

"Look at these," he said, handing Reese a stack of small-frame photographs. They looked like the pornography shots available on every other Saigon street corner, and he was not surprised when he saw bare flesh in the top photo. The bare flesh belonged to a young girl astride what looked to be the engorged penis of an American.

"You've taken up collecting beaver shots." Reese grinned. "How original."

Clifford didn't smile when he handed over a big Sherlock-Holmes-type magnifying glass. "Look at number four."

Reese found the photo with the red grease pencil number in the upper-right corner and focused the glass on it. "It's some guy getting a blow job."

"Look at the lower left-hand side of the shot," Clifford said.

Reese did as he was told and saw that the dark shape in the picture was apparently an American jungle fatigue jacket. With the glass, he could barely make out that it had a name tag sewn on it. "So?"

Clifford handed over a twenty-by-twenty-five-centimeter glossy blowup of the smaller picture. In the grainy enlargement, the name tag could be read, Johnso. The last letter was cut off by the frame of the photo, but the name had to be Johnson. "Who's Johnson and why do I give a shit if he got laid?"

"Look at the collar insignia."

Reese looked and saw the black shape of an oak leaf on the right collar; the left showed the crossed rifles of an infantry officer. "An infantry major, right?"

"A dead infantry major," Clifford's voice lost its monotone. "Johnson was one of the guys killed in the Chez Charles incident."

"But why do you think he was a leak?" Reese asked. "And if he was, why was he killed?"

Clifford snorted derisively. "He was obviously compromised. These are photos of him screwing a juvenile, and that's worth at least a few years in Leavenworth at any court-martial in town. What if he was confronted with these and talked to try to buy his way out?"

"But why would they have killed him?"

"Maybe they had gotten everything from him that they could and wasted him to shut him up."

"Where did you get this stuff?"

"By sheer accident," Clifford said. "The MPs popped a cowboy trying to peddle this stuff in front of the Cholon PX. Since the photos apparently showed an American officer involved in a sex act with a juvenile, they turned this guy over to CID. While they talked to him, the photo lab did the blowup and, when they saw Johnson's name tape, they called me. They've been ordered to call me with any leads they got about the Chez Charles hit and thought I'd be interested. I had them bring the Dink over here immediately, and I had a long talk with him about his wares."

Reese noticed that Clifford's wrinkled, sweated-out shirt had several small bloodstains on it that hadn't been there the last time he'd seen him.

"What did you find out?"

"This punk works for a Vietnamese publisher by the name of Do Pham Tran. Tran's pretty well connected—he even does printing for MACV. Apparently our cowboy has a habit of poking his nose into places where it don't belong, places like his employer's wall safe. Anyway, he found several sets of negatives like this in Tran's office and decided to go into business for himself selling porno prints."

"He didn't get greedy, though. He only took this one roll, figuring that after he printed it, he would replace it and borrow another one. He thought that Tran would never miss just one roll if he happened to check his safe. Anyway, he has a cousin who runs a darkroom, so they printed up several sets of that one roll, but he got policed up before he sold the first set of prints."

"Well, I'll be damned," Reese said. "I take back all the nasty things I was going to say to you this morning. What are we going to do now?"

"We're going to pay this guy's boss, Mr. Do Pham Tran, a little visit. I want to see what's in the rest of the negatives in that safe, and I want to ask this Tran a few pointed questions. Like why he took those pictures."

"When do we go?"

Clifford stood. "As soon as we can get our things together. When Santelli and Chief show up, get them ready to go."

"You got it."

SIMON HARRISON sipped his whiskey neat, his eyes scanning the people clustered around the rooftop bar of the Caravelle Hotel on Tu Do Street. Facing Le Loi Square, the Caravelle was the hangout for the Saigon press corps and the preferred watering hole for anyone who was anyone in town. That included the best-looking Western women in Saigon. Off-duty airline stewardesses, embassy secretaries, Red Cross girls and bored political wives all gathered at the Caravelle's bar. Though it wasn't yet noon, the bar was busy, and several serious seductions were already in progress.

When he didn't spot anyone interesting enough to leave his table to talk to, Harrison settled back to wait for Laura Winthrop. The well-washed safari jacket, faded suntan pants and worn chukka boots he wore clashed with the silk paisley ascot at his throat, but he thought it made him look the very picture of the war correspondent in the Hemingway grand tradition. The fact that he made a point of never going to the field to cover the fighting didn't bother him in the least. After all, hadn't Papa written most of his best stuff from the hotel bars in Spain? He also had to admit that the costume worked wonders with visiting airline stewardesses and virginal Red Cross girls.

As his eyes roved over the women, he wondered what would be on Laura's little mind that day. Not much, if he remembered correctly, but she had given him several rather memorable evenings. There was something terribly attractive about the fresh-scrubbed innocence of American girls. As a rule, they were so devoid of feminine artifice and so easy that it was difficult for him to think of them as being real women.

Laura, however, had almost been an exception to that rule. He'd had to work hard to get her, but the extra effort had been more than worth it. He sighed when he thought of her sleek thighs, taut belly and magnificent breasts, to say nothing of her thick, long blond mane. She was the finest example of Americana he had ever had the pleasure of. It was too bad really that he had not kept her around for a little while longer, but the call of unknown flesh had lured him away from her as it always did.

He had seen her several times since then at one press function or the other, and he had been pleased to see that she was holding her own in the dog-eat-dog world of the Saigon press corps. No one could say that Simon Harrison didn't know how to pick real talent.

Just then he looked over and saw Laura walk through the door onto the open rooftop. Most of the men at the bar saw her, too, and their eyes snapped to follow her the same as Harrison's did. She was more stunning than he had remembered, or maybe it was simply that he had not seen her in a while. The reporter sighed again. Maybe he should rethink his policy of never returning to the scene of one of his previous conquests. The movement of her lithe body under the thin dress and the mane of long blond hair framing her face was more than a little enticing.

He stood as she came up to the table and flashed her an easy smile. "Laura, how nice to see you again. How long has it been?"

She extended her hand and looked at him warmly. "Too long, Simon. It's good to see you, too."

He pulled out a chair for her and helped her sit down. "What can I get for you, my dear?"

"Campari, please."

Harrison made small talk until the waiter brought Laura's drink. "Now," he said. "What can I do for you other than enjoy the pleasure of your company?"

Laura shot a quick glance around the room before leaning across the table. Harrison's eyes automatically focused on her full breasts straining against the thin fabric of her dress. "Have you ever heard of someone called the Frenchman?"

Trying to hide his shock, Harrison leaned back and took another drink of his whiskey to buy time. Finally he answered her. "No, I can't say that I have. Why do you ask?"

"Simon, I'm on to something big, I just know it, and I need your help."

The thought flashed through his mind that only God could help Laura Winthrop now. She had said the magic word and, as in the fairy tale, once the word was spoken, it could never be taken back. "What is it that you're working on and how can I help?"

She looked around the rooftop again, the very picture of a movie spy. "I have a source..."

Harrison was startled, but managed to hide it well.

"And he mentioned something about someone called the Frenchman."

"Who is this man?" He hoped that he didn't sound too anxious. "And what did he say?"

"I have to protect him," she said apologetically. "You know how it is."

"I certainly do," he said. He didn't bother to add that he also knew she wanted to protect him because it was somebody she was sleeping with. Harrison knew that many men behaved like utter fools once a woman got them into her bed.

"Anyway," she continued, "he mentioned something about this man called the Frenchman, but when I asked him who he was, he wouldn't tell me anything about him—he just got secretive. The Frenchman sounded interesting, though, so I thought I'd ask you about him."

Harrison took a long drink. He thought that of all the curses of womankind, perhaps the most dangerous was their incurable curiosity. More good men have fallen because a woman got curious about something they said or did than for any other reason.

"Just what is this mysterious Frenchman supposed to be?"

"That's the problem," she admitted. "I really don't know. But I think he may be some kind of spy for the North Vietnamese."

Harrison laughed, mostly to relieve the tension he felt building inside him. "What are you planning to do, write a book?"

She smiled back at him. "No, I just thought that it might make a good story."

Jesus, Mary and Joseph! She thought that the Frenchman was just a good story? As Harrison knew only too well, that was a story that several governments would kill to have their hands on. But as Harrison also knew, the Frenchman was very particular about who knew about his business. He was even more particular about who knew his identity. Except for a small cadre of hard-core Vietcong agents like Harrison, the mere knowledge of the Frenchman's existence could be a death sentence.

"I'll ask around," Harrison said. "I know a lot of people in this town, and maybe I can pick up something for you."

Laura's face was all smiles as she reached across the table and took his hand. "Thank you so much, Simon, I knew I could count on you."

"I'm always glad to do anything I can to help you, Laura," he answered, and there was a note of near sadness in his voice.

9

August 17, Caravelle Hotel

Simon Harrison watched Laura walk across the rooftop with a sincere sadness in his eyes. When she disappeared around the corner, he signaled for the waiter to bring another drink. He knew that the Frenchman would want to know about this development instantly, but he didn't have the heart to make his report right away. He wanted to let Laura enjoy the rest of the day before he brought the long night down upon her.

When his drink came, a double, the British reporter knocked half of it back immediately before settling down to sip the remainder. What an odd turn of fate it was that made him seal the destiny of such a beautiful girl. But then, it had been another beautiful girl who had brought him to where he was now. Like Laura, she too had been cursed with an overabundance of feminine curiosity.

Harrison had been young back then, barely sixteen, when the squire's daughter in his small English village had chosen him to exercise her curiosity on. He had been the son of the local brewer and initially had been afraid of her. In the English society of his day, brewers' sons did not dally with the daughters of the gentry. But she had persisted, and in the end he had succumbed. When you are a sixteen-year-old boy, hormones will win out every time.

They were caught in the act, as it were, and the girl cried rape. Rather than take him in front of the magistrate, which would have tarnished the girl's reputation forever, the squire had taken the matter into his own hands. With the help of two of his retainers, Harrison had been beaten within an inch of his life and told that he would be killed if he remained in the village another day.

The nearest city to his village had been London, but the postwar British capital had been no place for a homeless teenage boy. With the demobilization of the World War II British forces, there had been no work for him and, with the chronic housing shortage left over from the blitz, there was no place for him to stay even if he'd had enough money to rent a room.

As it was, what little money he had, he rationed out to stave off hunger. But it ran out after a couple of weeks on the street. He nicked a shiny red apple from a greengrocers stall one afternoon and while making his high-speed escape ran straight into the man delivering bundles of newspapers at the corner news vendor's stall.

After finding out what was going on, the man paid the angry grocer for the apple and talked him out of getting the police involved in the matter. More importantly, after hearing the young Harrison's story, he offered him a job working for his leftist newspaper, the *Daily Worker,* and a place to sleep in his home.

By the time he was eighteen, Harrison had risen to being in charge of distributing the papers throughout London's east side. His quick head for figures and problem-solving abilities caught the attention of the paper's circulation manager. When he was asked what he wanted to do with the rest of his life, the young Harrison answered that he wanted to become a reporter. Arrangements were made for Harrison to complete his education at the paper's expense while he worked as an apprentice reporter.

As he rose in his newfound profession, he never forgot the kindness the Communists had shown him. When he became a full-fledged reporter, they asked him to repay that kindness and he had been more than willing to help in any way he could. The Communists' dream of a classless society where young working-class boys couldn't be beaten to death at the whim of an angry upper-class father appealed greatly to him. He immediately applied for membership in the British Communist party.

By now, however, he had no youthful illusions about international communism. He was well aware that the classless society they talked about was so much bullshit, as the Yankees put it. But where he had been denied admittance to the higher social ranks in England because of his birth, as a card-carrying Communist he was a part of the privileged elite.

With that high status, however, came equally high responsibilities, and one of his responsibilities in Saigon was to be an operative for the Frenchman. His direct contact with the Communist agent was through

Do Pham Tran, a Vietnamese publisher. Tran, however, was more than merely a publisher; he was the half brother of Lucian de Champ, the man better known only as the Frenchman.

Born to the Vietnamese mistress of the elder de Champ, Tran had taken after his mother and showed no signs of his French heritage. When the two half brothers had still been in school, Tran had taken his mother's family name. When de Champ took over the family rubber plantations, Tran moved to Saigon. Beyond the accident of birth, the only tie between the two brothers was the fact that they were both devoted Communists. While de Champ ran his operations from the old family villa in Cambodia, Tran worked for the cause from the Vietnamese capital.

Tran's wealth allowed him access to the upper echelons of Vietnamese society, and his publishing business gave him many American contacts, as well. One of his more lucrative contracts was to print the posters for MACV that warned American soldiers about the dangers of venereal disease. There was real irony in that since the real source of Tran's wealth was his ownership of some of Vietnam's better bordellos.

The Frenchman knew the value of having eyes and ears in the small rooms where sexually frustrated Americans worked off their lusts on the willing bodies of Vietnamese girls. Furthermore, Tran's establishments were not the assembly-line whorehouses that serviced GIs from the DMZ to the Delta. Tran's places were true houses of pleasure where nothing was impossible. In fact, the more unique the request, the more willing Tran was to fill it, particularly when the man making the request was a high-ranking American officer.

South Vietnamese officials also frequented Tran's establishments, but their tastes were more difficult to cater to. They lusted after big-breasted blond Western women, which was why the Frenchman was a major player in the Asian white-slave business. Most of his Caucasian girls were imported from Europe and Mexico, Western tourists who were already addicted to the drugs that would keep them enslaved while they serviced Asian men. Tran prospered because he was discreet and because he fulfilled dreams. He also prospered because the information he gathered from his sexual dream factories was some of the best Intelligence the VC received.

That was how Tran had learned that MACV-SOG was closing in on his half brother, the Frenchman. One of the officers who had died with Lieutenant Colonel Simpton had been a man with a strong taste for forbidden flesh, and the younger the better. More than that, however, he'd had a bad habit of talking to his young bed partners while they were servicing him.

This major had foolishly thought that he was all alone with his little playmates when he delivered his monologues about his frustrations with his job. After all, a twelve-year-old Vietnamese girl would never understand a word he said. But the tape recorder did. Regardless of the high fees Tran's madames received to insure strict privacy, every room was bugged and the more interesting encounters were also photographed for the record.

Along with being a good Intelligence-gathering tool, Tran considered his photographs to be insurance in case anything ever went wrong and he needed friends in high places. Were he to find himself desperately needing a friend, the threat of exposing the photographs was sure to get positive results.

"WHY ARE WE DOING THIS all by ourselves?" Reese asked as he checked the magazine in the bottom of his Swedish K. "Where are all the usual players, the MI, CID and the rest of your little spook buddies?"

Santelli also wanted to know the answer to his captain's question. Moving against a suspected VC cell as big as this one wasn't a job for four men, particularly four men with no backup. They should have had some heavy firepower backing this kind of play.

Clifford was in no mood to put up with Reese's jabs about the CIA this morning. He was well into a serious sleep deficit and was running on pure adrenaline.

"If you haven't figured it out," the CIA agent snapped, "somebody's been passing information to the Dinks about this operation. So far, there's been a friendly body count of six and one of them was a top Company asset. I've got my ass in a crack, and I'm not letting another swinging dick in on this thing until I can get some idea of just what is going on around here. *Capisce?*"

"That's supposed to be my line," Santelli said with a grin, trying to break the tension.

Clifford spun on him. "And you watch your mouth, LT. The only reason you're here is that you're too fucking stupid to get involved with treason."

Santelli bristled instantly and started for the CIA man.

"That's about enough, Clifford!" Reese stepped in between the two men, and Santelli backed off. "The only reason either one of us are here is because this investigation affects Jan Snow. If it hadn't been for the attack on him, you'd be doing this stunt all by your lonesome. We don't have to be here, and the next time you give either one of us any more of your shit, we're gone and we'll take our chances with the Frenchman from Dak Sang. *Capisce?*"

The CIA man backed down quickly. He looked properly sheepish as he reached up to rub his red-rimmed eyes. "Look, guys," he said. "It's been a long last couple of days. With Sylvan getting himself wasted, I've had a lot on my plate lately and I really need your help on this one. If we can pop this Tran guy and wring him out, I think we'll finally have a handle on the Frenchman."

Reese caught Clifford's use of the plural and backed down, too. "Okay," he said. "Let's just get it done and we can argue about it later. Deal?"

Clifford nodded. "Let's go."

THE SIGN on the front of the cinder-block building at the corner of Lu Toi and Lam Son streets read ABC Printing And Publishing in English, French and Viet-namese. Judging by the size of the building, Tran was doing well with his printing business and whatever else he had going on the side. Reese drove the jeep past the building and pulled into an alley in the middle of the block. Reaching down for the short piece of chain welded to the jeep's frame, he looped it through the rim of the steering wheel and padlocked it tightly. Leaving an unlocked vehicle in this part of Saigon was an open invitation to theft.

The four men stepped out of the jeep and quickly checked their weapons. The Indian sniper had traded in his sniper's rifle for a CAR-15, and the stubby submachine gun looked out of place in his hands.

"Work your way around to the back," Reese told Santelli and Chief. "I'll give you fifteen minutes. Remember, we don't want the White Mice getting in on this, so once you're inside, move fast, flush it out, but don't let things get out of hand. I don't want us to be in there a minute longer than we have to."

Holding their weapons low and lined up with their bodies, Santelli and the sniper moved up the alley until they reached the open space behind the row of buildings facing the street. They immediately turned left around the corner and disappeared from sight.

As Reese and Clifford waited, the Special Forces officer kept an eye out for street kids keeping an eye on them. If Tran was a Vietcong agent, he would be certain to have a warning system set up using the kids to watch the streets for signs of trouble. So far, though, Reese had not seen any shoeshine boys furtively ducking into Tran's building.

"That's it," Clifford said, impatiently glancing down at his watch. "Let's do him."

Keeping their weapons down at their sides, the two men hurried up the street to the front door. A bell tinkled when the door opened and they rushed inside, their weapons at the ready. Reese pushed past the reception counter to the open door of the office. Inside, a portly middle-aged Vietnamese man was reaching to close the wall safe when Clifford and Reese burst in on him. His eyes grew wide at the sight of their weapons, but he didn't try to run. "Do Pham Tran?" Clifford snapped.

The man nodded slightly, and Clifford rushed him. Without another word being spoken, the CIA agent cuffed Tran's hands behind his back, slapped a strip of tape over his mouth, tied a blindfold around his eyes and forced him into the chair by the desk.

A second later Santelli and Chief came in from the back room herding three more terrified Vietnamese men with their hands held up over their heads. "These guys were running a printing press in the back," the LT said. "The rest of the building's clean."

"Stack 'em over against the wall."

Santelli motioned with the barrel of his CAR, and the printers squatted on the floor against the wall. Clifford immediately went for the wall safe and started pawing through its contents. Behind a pile of what looked like legal papers and several stacks of Vietnamese currency and American MPC, he found a cigar box full of 35 mm film canisters. Opening one of them, he took out a roll of negatives and, unrolling the end, held it up to the light from the window.

"Bingo!" he said triumphantly. "Here's more of that stuff. We've got him."

While Clifford rummaged through the wall safe, Reese started collecting the papers from Tran's desk drawers. "I need a box to put this stuff in," he told Chief.

The sniper ducked back into the press room and returned with two cardboard boxes. Reese then tossed the jeep padlock keys to Chief. "Get the jeep and bring it around to the front."

A minute later the papers were packed and Reese was ready to go. "What are we going to do with them?" he asked, looking over at the three Vietnamese workers sitting against the base of the wall.

Clifford barely spared the printers a glance as he cleaned out the last of the safe's contents. "Kick their asses out in the street," he said.

Santelli opened the door and motioned with the muzzle of his CAR. *"Di di,"* he snapped.

The Vietnamese leaped to their feet and were running before they reached the door.

Grabbing Tran under the arms, Reese and Santelli frog marched him out to the waiting jeep and, lifting him over the side of the vehicle, dropped him in the rear seat. Clifford brought the boxes of papers out and dumped them in the back as Reese slid into the driver's seat, slammed into first gear and popped the clutch. With a squeak of the rear tires, they were on their way.

The entire operation had taken less than five minutes.

10

August 17, Cholon

Back at the safehouse, Clifford didn't waste any time going to work on Tran. Rather than using the well-proven traditional but time-consuming methods of intimidation and physical interrogation, he went completely modern. As soon as the Vietnamese was strapped down to the table in the soundproof interrogation room on the first floor, Clifford called in a man with a hypodermic syringe.

"The miracle of modern chemistry," he said as he watched the medic insert a saline IV drip into Tran's arm. As soon as the needle was in place, he injected a mixture of sodium thiopental, scopolamine and a touch of LSD into the drip bag. The mixture would break down a man's resistance much more quickly than a rubber hose or electric shock. While the information from a man under the drug's influence was sometimes a bit garbled, it would be what he really knew, not what he thought his interrogators wanted to hear.

"It takes a few minutes to start working," the medic explained as he put a blood pressure cuff around Tran's other arm. The chemical interrogation sometimes caused an adverse reaction in some prisoners, so the room was equipped with the oxygen, adrenaline and the antidote needed to bring a man around if he couldn't take the drug.

The drugs immediately put Tran into a light trance-like state. His eyes were shut, but Reese could see them moving under his closed lids as he tried to follow the patterns he saw in his mind. The medic took his pulse and nodded. His patient was ready.

Clifford turned on a small Japanese tape recorder and positioned the microphone to catch everything Tran said. "Tell me about the photos in your safe," the CIA agent asked. "Where did you get them?"

There was a blissful expression on Tran's face as he answered, "They come from the boom-boom houses. I have cameras there."

"Who do you take pictures of?"

Tran giggled like a child. "Many Yankee with girl. And sometime with boy, too."

"Which Yankees?"

"Only important men."

"Tell me about the photos you took of Major Ralph Johnson."

"Major Johnson—" Tran smiled slowly "—he the one who like the young girl too much. He talk to them *beaucoup* and I listen all time when he talk. Major Johnson good talker."

"What did he talk about?"

"He say the Yankees they want to kill the Frenchman, but they no can find him." Tran smiled broadly and giggled again. "They no can find today, they no can find tomorrow. He not in Vietnam."

"Where is the Frenchman?"

Tran continued to smile. "I no can tell you. It big secret. *Beaucoup* big."

Clifford stepped closer to him. "Where is he?" he repeated insistently.

"I no can tell you now," Tran answered, his voice slowing and dragging the words out. "No can tell you..."

Tran slumped against the straps holding him to the tabletop. The medic bent over and checked his heart with his stethoscope. "He's okay," he said, looking back up at Clifford. "He's just out of it. I must have given him a little too much. I'll cut the dose next time."

"Hell!" Clifford slammed his hand on the table. "Now we'll have to wait an hour or two before he wakes up again."

"We did get a confirmation about Johnson, though," Reese said.

"But we didn't get the name of the other bastards who've been running their mouths off while they're getting laid." Clifford ran his hand through his short-cropped hair. "This stuff works, but sometimes it takes a little while to get what you need."

"While he's out," Reese said, "maybe I should start going over those papers we collected from his office...there might be something in there we can use."

"Good idea," Clifford replied. "I'll get our linguist to help you with them."

THE RAID HAD GONE so well that neither Reese nor Clifford realized the serious mistake they had made. One of the printers they had turned loose at Tran's shop was a Vietcong agent, a courier. The first thing the man did when he reached the street was get to a phone and put in a call to Simon Harrison.

When he heard about Tran's capture, Harrison's heart sank. The reporter had no romantic ideas about Tran's ability to withstand interrogation by the CIA, and he knew more about the Frenchman than anyone. The Americans did not go in for the barbaric practice of torturing information out of prisoners, but their methods of chemical interrogation were every bit as effective, if not more so. The only good thing was that if what he had heard about the American interrogation drugs was true, it would take a while for them to get any information. And even to get that, they would have to ask exactly the right questions.

Harrison didn't have any idea why the Americans had picked up Tran. His long-established cover should have been bulletproof, but the reason really didn't matter now that he was in their hands. The only way to salvage anything from the situation was to get him released as soon as possible, and only the Frenchman could do that.

He quickly put in a call to a number in Long Bien, right outside of Saigon. When the call was answered, the reporter started talking in Vietnamese to the man at the other end about the fishing in the Saigon River. Vietnamese is a poetic language, and no one listening in would have thought there was anything unusual about two men talking about the sharks who had captured the king fish's little brother.

It was an awkward way to communicate, but it was foolproof. Even if someone had been listening in, they would have learned nothing. Like most of the expatriate Brits around the world, Harrison spoke the local language well and could fool everyone but a native.

An hour later Harrison received a call from the Frenchman. From the quality of the sound, he knew that it was patched through from a radiophone, the only way de Champ ever communicated with him. The fact that the Frenchman had risked a call at all told Harrison how seriously de Champ regarded this latest development.

The Frenchman's response was exactly what Harrison had expected from him—cold but controlled rage. Even though the two half brothers had lived most of their adult lives apart, the tie between them was strong. As the elder, de Champ still felt very protective of his younger, half-Vietnamese sibling. In fact, by capturing Tran, Clifford had accidentally stumbled onto the Frenchman's only real weakness, and a secret weakness at that.

To the people he came in contact with, either the Vietcong, drug smugglers or black marketers, Lucian de Champ appeared so cold and controlled that many wondered if he were completely human. He had never been seen to express an emotion, but then, very few people had ever seen him around his younger brother.

As a child de Champ had often fled the strict, sterile environment of his father's villa to go to the cozy warmth of the small house nearby, where Tran's mother lived. The Vietnamese love children, and the young French boy had been welcomed by his father's mistress. Though he was not her child, she treated him as if he were and lavished love, warmth and affection on him. In Lucian's young mind, this Vietnamese woman and her baby son had become his real family. He had to live in the big villa, but his heart stayed with his adopted Vietnamese family.

When he later learned that Tran was his half brother, they became even more inseparable. Because of what he saw as the injustice of French colonial rule of Indochina, Lucian became a Communist and brought Tran into the movement, as well. With the fall of the French in 1954, Lucian stayed on at the family estate in Cambodia while Tran moved to Saigon to work for the cause. Since then, they had rarely visited each other, but Lucian de Champ had never forgotten the childhood ties that had been forged between him and his Vietnamese half brother.

Harrison was not all that surprised at the orders he received over the phone. He knew that Laura had been doomed from the instant that the Frenchman's name passed her lips, but he had not thought that de Champ would want to become personally involved with her fate. Harrison didn't claim to have an inside line to the Frenchman's psyche, but as an only child, he had always wanted to have a brother—a brother who would have come to his rescue at his hour of need as de Champ was trying to rescue Tran. Somehow it seemed fitting.

Harrison was greatly relieved, however, that he had not been ordered to personally kill Laura. He had killed on orders from his party superiors before and he had even killed women on occasion. But it would have been very difficult for him to kill Laura. This way he could lie to himself and say that he had only turned her over to the Frenchman. He would never see her again, and the Frenchman would never mention her, so his conscience at least would be clean.

He knew, however, that was mere sophistry. Once she was in the Frenchman's custody, the world would never see Laura Winthrop again, dead or alive. The only good thing was that the Frenchman was a civilized man, and Laura would not be mistreated before she died. Once she had served her purpose, she would simply be killed, quickly and efficiently, and her body buried in an unmarked grave.

Her disappearance would be a three-day wonder in Saigon, but little more than that. Even though the CIA would know what had happened to her, there was no way that they would release the information.

While he still had the courage, he dialed another number. "United Press," the voice on the other end of the line said.

"May I speak to Laura Winthrop, please."

There was a pause while he was connected, then he heard her husky voice.

"This is Simon, I have some good news for you."

UNDER THE TREES lining the street bordering the Saigon racetrack in the northwest side of the city, Simon

PLAY THE

CARNIVAL WHEEL

LUCKY

scratch-off game
and get as many as
FIVE FREE GIFTS...

HOW TO PLAY:

1. With a coin, carefully scratch off the silver area at right. Then check your number against the chart below to find out which gifts you're eligible to receive. If you're lucky, you'll instantly be entitled to receive two or more books and possibly another gift, ABSOLUTELY FREE!

2. Send back this card and we'll promptly send you any Free Gifts you're entitled to. You'll receive brand-new, red-hot Gold Eagle® books and possibly a terrific Surprise Mystery Gift!

3. We're betting you'll want more of these action-packed stories, so unless you tell us otherwise, we'll send you four more high-voltage books every other month to preview. They're guaranteed to be the best of today's action adventure fiction! The four books are yours for only $13.80*—that's a saving of over 10% off the cover prices. Always delivered right to your home. And always at a discount off the cover price!

4. Your satisfaction is guaranteed! You may return any shipment of books and cancel at any time. The Free Books and Gift remain yours to keep!

NO COST! NO RISK!
NO OBLIGATION TO BUY!

FREE SURPRISE MYSTERY GIFT!

IT COULD BE YOURS FREE WHEN YOU PLAY THE LUCKY "CARNIVAL WHEEL."

CLAIM YOUR FREE GIFTS! MAIL THIS CARD TODAY!

PRINTED IN THE U.S.A.

GOLD EAGLE NO BLUFF, NO RISK GUARANTEE

- You're not required to buy a single book—ever!
- Even as a subscriber, you must be completely satisfied, or you may return any shipment of books at our cost and cancel your subscription.
- The Free Books and Gift you receive from this ''Carnival Wheel'' offer remain yours to keep—in any case!

If offer card is missing, write to: Gold Eagle Reader Service, 3010 Walden Avenue, P.O. Box 1867, Buffalo, NY 14269-1867

◀ MAIL THIS CARD TODAY! ◀

Harrison waited impatiently for Laura Winthrop to show up. Part of him hoped that for once she was not going to be fashionably late. He had to get past the ARVN roadblocks leading out of Saigon before dark. But another part of him, however, hoped against hope that she would not appear at all.

A blue-and-yellow Renault Saigon taxicab came down the street, and Harrison stepped back under a tree. There had been no horse racing at the track since Tet and little reason for a taxi to use this particular side street. When the cab pulled over to the curb at the other end of the track, he knew that it was Laura.

As he had instructed her, she stopped the cab short of their meeting place and waited until it was out of sight before hurrying toward him. Her long blond hair was tied up, and even though the sun was going down, sunglasses covered her blue eyes. She had dressed sensibly for the trip in pants, a light windbreaker and chukka boots. She was ready for the grand adventure of her life, but she had no idea it was to be the last adventure she would ever have.

"Laura!" Harrison said, quickly glancing around to make sure that no one was watching them. "Does anyone know that you're here?"

She shook her head. "No, you said not to tell anyone."

"Good. Come quickly."

"Where are we going?"

"I found out who the Frenchman is and I've arranged for you to have an interview with him."

Laura was stunned. "You're kidding!"

Harrison smiled. "No."

Impulsively she threw her arms around his neck. "Oh Simon, thank you."

"Come on, my dear, we have to hurry."

Laura was so enthused with the prospect of the interview that she didn't stop to ask herself a few critical questions as she followed him into the car parked by the curb. Questions such as how was it that he was able to get a handle on the elusive Frenchman so fast when the CIA couldn't find him? And, even more importantly, why was he willing to give an interview to an American reporter?

Had she been thinking more clearly, Laura would have asked herself these questions, as any reporter with half a brain would have. But she wanted this story so badly that she had turned off the logic centers of her brain and was running on pure ambition.

CLIFFORD'S FACE WAS grim when Reese walked into his office. "What's up?" the SF officer asked.

"I just got a phone call," the CIA agent said. "Do you know a woman named Laura Winthrop?"

Reese froze for an instant, all his instincts telling him that something was wrong, terribly wrong. "Yes, I do," he said cautiously. "Why?"

"So does the Frenchman," Clifford answered. "And right now, he's holding her hostage."

"Oh God, no."

"Who is she?"

"A girl I've been seeing for the past couple of months. I've been staying with her here in town."

"Who is she?"

"She's a reporter for UPI."

"What in the hell did you think you were doing with her?" Clifford exploded. "For Christ's sake, Reese, sleeping with a fucking reporter. That's got to be the stupidest thing I've..."

Reese's fist slammed Clifford's head back with a snap. He fell back down into his swivel chair, stunned. "Shit!" he said softly, feeling his jaw to see if it was broken. "I'm sorry, man. I didn't know you felt that way about her."

"If it's any help," Reese said truthfully, rubbing the knuckles of his right hand, "I didn't know, either, until right now."

Neither man spoke for a long moment until Reese broke the silence. "What does he want for her?"

Clifford winced as he ran his finger along his split lip. "He wants our man Tran in exchange."

"The porno connection?"

Clifford nodded. "Yeah."

"Why?"

"Fucked if I know."

"Don't you think we'd better find out first?"

"The thought had occurred to me," Clifford said. "Let's go have another talk with Tran."

Reese beat him to the door.

11

August 17, Laura's Apartment

Reese felt strange opening the door to Laura's apartment knowing that she wasn't there and wouldn't be back for some time, if ever. The place still held a hint of her scent, but it felt lifeless.

When he and Clifford had gone back to interrogate Tran again, they had gotten nothing from him about the Frenchman and why he had kidnapped Laura. Every time Clifford mentioned Laura, the Vietnamese seemed not to know who she was and started talking about the girls in his whorehouses again. Except for the names of several more American officers who frequented his establishments and had unwittingly passed sensitive information to their bed partners, he had said little of value to the investigation.

After an hour of fruitless questioning, Reese had called it an evening and had driven over to Laura's place to see if she had left any clues behind that might point to why she had been captured. So far, though, there was no sign that there had been a struggle in the apartment; not a single thing was out of place. It looked as though she had walked out on her own as if to go to work. Even the breakfast coffee cups were stacked in the kitchen sink.

He crossed the front room to her desk and snapped on the lamp. Lying in the middle of the desk was a large envelope bearing his name on the front in block letters. He ripped it open, and several black-and-white Polaroid photographs spilled out. They showed Laura with a masked Vietnamese man on either side of her holding on to her arms. The men were dressed in black pajama uniforms and were carrying AK-47s. Laura was in the hands of the Vietcong.

There was a piece of paper in the envelope. Reese took it out and saw that it was also addressed to him. The note was short and to the point. If Reese wanted to see Laura alive again, he would be at a certain street corner at ten o'clock that night. He would also be alone and unarmed or he would be killed on the spot.

He dropped the note next to the Polaroids and took a deep breath. What in hell had Laura gotten herself into this time? How did she ever get into the Frenchman's hands?

His mind flashed back to the night after he had come back from that fiasco in the Straight Edge Woods. He remembered that he'd had his briefcase with him that evening, and the CIA sanction against the Frenchman had been in the briefcase. But try as he could, he could not remember if he had locked the briefcase. He could, however, remember how curious she had been about how he had been hurt and what he was working on. But given her curiosity, she had not tried to wheedle the information out of him after he had indicated that he couldn't talk about it. That was not in character for her, but he had been so pissed off about the failed mission that he had taken little notice of it.

He also remembered that he had drunk most of a bottle of brandy that evening and, after making love, had slept the sleep of the dead. She could have gotten up in the night and gone through the briefcase and he would not have woken up. Hell, as drunk as he had been, a North Vietnamese infantry company could have marched right through the bedroom and he wouldn't have noticed it.

She had also been unnaturally quiet at breakfast that next morning. But he had been so hung over that he hadn't given it much thought, either. Her uncharacteristic silence could have been the result of her having read the documents in the briefcase and being disturbed by their contents. If she had read them, she would have tried to follow up on the information. The story behind the CIA sanction would have been too tantalizing for her to pass up.

He knew he was making a great leap in logic with no real facts to base his conclusions on, but he had seen Laura in action before. He knew the depths of her ambition and how hard she worked when she thought she had her teeth into a real lead. The twisted path she had followed to doggedly track down the SOG story had proven that she could develop a story from mere hints and rumors. If she had seen the sanction, she'd had more than hints and rumors to work on; she would have had solid facts, and following them up could have led her into this mess.

The big question now was what was he going to do about the invitation from the Frenchman. If she had gotten involved because of what she had read in his briefcase, then he owed it to her to try to extricate her. The next question was, however, would giving himself up to the Frenchman help her or make matters even worse?

There was only one way he was going to find out. He reached for the phone on Laura's desk and called the hotel where Santelli was staying.

LAURA TRIED AGAIN to find a comfortable place to sit on the steel floor of the American three-quarter-ton truck as it slowly bumped along a badly rutted road. But with her hands and feet bound, it was difficult. She was battered and ached all over from the repeated pounding she was receiving. She had no idea where she was and, since she was blindfolded and couldn't look at her watch, she had lost all sense of time. She had the impression, however, that she had been in the truck for at least two hours.

The ride to the outskirts of Saigon with Simon had been strange. He had been unusually quiet all the way and had not answered any of her questions about the interview. When they reached the first ARVN checkpoint on the road to Cu Chi, however, he turned on the old Simon Harrison charm as he presented the South Vietnamese NCO with a typewritten pass that quickly let him through.

"How did you get that after-hours pass?" she had asked after the ARVN waved them on. "I thought those were hard to come by."

Harrison smiled weakly. "I have good contacts in high places, my dear."

Less than half an hour later Laura figured out that she was in deep kimchee, as Mike Reese would have said. In fact, from the instant when Simon had slowed the car and pulled off onto a side road, she had felt uneasy. When she saw the two figures in black pajamas step out with AK-47 assault rifles held at the ready, she had known that something was wrong, dead wrong.

"Simon," she said as the car braked to a stop. "Those men, they're Vietcong."

The reporter turned to face her. "I know, my dear. They are going to take you to the Frenchman."

She studied his face for a moment, and when he couldn't look her in the eye, she was certain. "You're working for them, aren't you?"

He switched off the engine and was silent for a moment. "Yes, Laura, I am."

"But why, Simon. Why you?"

He opened the door and stepped out of the car. "It's a long story, my dear, but not half as interesting as the one the Frenchman will tell you when you see him."

She looked around frantically to see if there was anywhere she could run. But before she could move, one of the VC stepped up, the muzzle of his AK pointed at her, and, taking her arm, pulled her from the car. All thoughts of resistance faded as the man led her away. The last she had seen of Simon Harrison, he was sitting in the car staring out the windshield.

The truck stopped again, and the driver switched the engine off. From the sounds she heard, they had to be somewhere in the jungle. She heard a low conversation in what she thought was Vietnamese, and the truck started up again. The road immediately got rougher, and she felt that they were going uphill. Wherever the Frenchman was, she had a feeling that it was not in South Vietnam.

So far, she had been able to control her fear, but now it washed over her as she huddled on the floor of the truck. She tried not to cry, but tears formed under the blindfold. Mike had tried to warn her about trying to follow these kinds of stories, and she should have listened to him. There was a part of this war that was better left alone.

SANTELLI COULDN'T BELIEVE his ears. He had been fully dressed and waiting to go into action when Reese showed up at his door. Now that he had heard what his captain wanted to do, however, he was stunned. "You're completely out of your rabbit-assed mind, *Dai Uy*. You can't give yourself up to that French bastard. If he gets his hands on you, man, he's going to kill you dead."

Reese's eyes showed that the thought had occurred to him, as well. "I know," he said calmly as he paced the floor. "But I've got to go anyway."

"For Christ's sakes, why?"

Reese didn't answer for a moment. "Because I think I helped get her into this mess," he said. "And I hope I can get her out."

"What in the hell are you talking about?"

"For one thing, I was in the team that snatched Tran, and if the Frenchman's people have been watching our operation like Clifford thinks, I led them to her by staying at her place. Second, there's a good chance that she saw the CIA sanction I was carrying on him."

Santelli was stunned.

"I had it in my briefcase when I stayed at her place," Reese said. "And I don't think I had the briefcase locked. It's possible that she read it while I was asleep and thinks that she's on to a big story."

Reese didn't have to tell Santelli how many times Laura had talked about needing a big story to make her break into the ranks of serious war correspondents. The XO had been a part of her previous attempt to get the MACV-SOG story into print, and he knew the blond reporter was every bit as ambitious as she was good-looking.

"Oh, sweet Jesus," Santelli said softly.

"That's what I thought," Reese commented dryly. "Anyway, the only thing I can think of doing to help her is to go along with their demand and hope they take me to where she is."

"But why did he kidnap Laura?"

"The way I figure it," Reese said, "is that Tran's the key to this thing. The spooks have been after the Frenchman for years, and he's never done anything like this before. Suddenly we grab this Tran guy, and he goes nuts. Somehow we've really gotten into his shorts on this one, and the real question is why he's reacting this way.''

Santelli's jaw was set. "We can sure as hell go back and have another little chat with that Dink.''

"Do that," Reese said. "But don't do it until I've had a chance to surrender first. Clifford is going to shit a brick as it is.''

"You're making a big mistake, man." Santelli shook his head slowly.

"I know." Reese nodded. "But I'm going to do it anyway. I don't want him to kill her.''

Santelli snorted. "Uh-huh, this way, *Dai Uy* he's just going to kill both of you instead.''

"I don't think so," Reese said. "At least not right away. And I think I can buy enough time for you and Clifford to find out what's going on here. Remember, we have something he seems to want badly—Tran— and I don't think he'll do us until he has Tran back.''

"But why does he want that little bastard?" Santelli asked. "That's what I can't figure out.''

"I don't know, but I'm betting that Tran has the answers we're looking for.''

"You sure are betting," Santelli said. "You're betting your life on it.''

"What I'm betting on," Reese replied, "is that you'll be able to squeeze that pimp dry, find out what's going down and bail my ass out before he wastes me.''

"Jesus, *Dai Uy*—" Santelli shook his head slowly "—you're taking a big chance. What if we can't get to you in time?"

"All I'm asking is that you try."

"You've got my word on that," Santelli promised. "And I'll keep my boot up Clifford's ass till we learn something."

"That's good enough for me."

"When are you going?"

Reese glanced down at his watch. "Just a few minutes. The meeting's scheduled for 2200 hours."

"That's the curfew time," Santelli said.

"I know. They obviously picked it because the streets will be empty and no one will see what goes down."

"Well," Reese said as he headed for the door, "I've got to get on it."

"Good luck," Santelli said. They were empty words this time, but he had to say them anyway.

"Catch you later."

REESE PULLED the jeep over to the curb, switched it off and killed the lights. He was a few minutes early, but that was better than being late. He used the chain to lock the steering wheel even though he knew that ten minutes after he left the jeep, some Vietnamese kid with a pair of bolt cutters would unlock it, hot-wire it and drive it off. A jeep was worth better than a year's salary on the black market.

He got out and stood quietly by the vehicle, his arms at his sides and his empty hands in clear sight in the dim light of the streetlight. He was certain that he was under observation, and the last thing he needed at that point was for his would-be kidnappers to think he was concealing a weapon. If he scared them off, it could easily turn into an assassination instead of a kidnapping. Killing him would probably serve the Frenchman's purposes just as well as his being taken prisoner. But it wouldn't do anything to help Laura, to say nothing of what it would do to him.

As he stood in the semidarkness, a shadow detached itself from the darkened building across the street and dashed to his side of the road. The dark figure was joined by two more and they slowly moved toward him. He forced himself to stand stock-still and tried to control his breathing. It was going down and he didn't want to spook them.

Two of the figures approached him, and Reese saw that they both had Tokarev pistols in their hands. The third figure stood back, covering them with an AK. The first man halted a few feet away and kept the pistol trained on him as his partner moved in closer. Reese forced himself to remain motionless as the second VC patted him down for weapons. When the VC found that he was clean, he backed away and said something to the first man.

"Mau di!" the man with the Tokarev said, motioning him back into the shadows.

Reese did as he was told and quickly walked toward the VC with the AK. As soon as he was off the street, his hands were tied behind his back and a blindfold placed over his eyes. Reese had always feared being captured by the Vietnamese and had to force himself not to panic. His plan had sounded good when he had discussed it with Santelli, but he had a sinking feeling that he had just done the most stupid thing in his entire life. And if he was right, it would be a very short life.

12

August 18, Cholon

To say that Dick Clifford was pissed would have been a serious understatement. When Santelli reported to him first thing in the morning that Reese had surrendered to the Frenchman, the CIA man exploded in fury. "Jesus Christ!" he yelled. "What the hell's wrong with him? That's the stupidest thing I've ever heard of!"

He shook his head in stunned disbelief. "Now the fucking Frenchman has two hostages."

Santelli stood quietly and let Clifford rant and rage for several minutes before cutting in. "Reese did say that he thought we'd find out what this is all about if we talk to Tran again. He's convinced that he's the key to this whole operation."

"Is he, now?" Clifford rested his head in his hands. "A fat lot of good that's going to do him now." He stared at his desktop and took a deep breath. "I wish I'd never met you fucking Green Berets. I was doing okay till I ran into you two assholes."

"Are you finished?" Santelli asked.

Clifford nodded dully but did not move.

"Can we talk to Tran now?"

Slowly Clifford got up from his chair. "Yeah, I guess so. This operation can't get any more fucked-up than it already is."

Santelli followed the CIA agent to the cell where Tran had been kept overnight. The Vietnamese was still groggy from the drugs and seemed disoriented. He was given a light breakfast and led to the latrine before being taken back into the interrogation room and strapped down again.

"Fire him up," Clifford told the medic. "But be careful with the dosage. I want some answers out of the dickhead this time."

The medic inserted the IV drip needle into Tran's arm and injected his chemical mixture into the IV bag. In seconds the Vietnamese was submerged in a trance.

Once again Tran seemed not to know who Laura Winthrop was when Clifford asked about her. He confused her with one of the whores working for him. Frustrated at being blocked on that avenue, the CIA man changed his line of questioning. "Do you work for the Frenchman?"

Upon hearing the spy's nickname, Tran switched to speaking French. Clifford had studied the language in college and was able to follow right along as Tran babbled. Santelli had also picked up some French, so he wasn't completely lost.

"Tell me about the spy called the Frenchman," Clifford insisted, cutting into a stream of gossipy information about expatriate French in Saigon. "Do you pass information to him?"

"Lucian," Tran sobbed. "I am sorry, my brother. I am very sorry."

"Who is Lucian?" Clifford bent over him, his voice low and insistent.

Tran seemed not to hear the question and continued babbling in French. "Harrison, my friend, tell Lucian that I am sorry."

"Who is Harrison?" the CIA man almost shouted.

"The long-nosed reporter," Tran answered in English. "He is my friend. He will help me. He will tell Lucian that I am sorry."

Something clicked in Clifford's brain. A look of astonishment passed over his face as he straightened up. "I'll be goddamned," he said softly. "I think I know who he's talking about."

"Who?"

"Simon fucking Harrison." Clifford almost spit the man's name. "That's who."

"Who's he?"

"He's a Commie-loving Brit bastard who works for the leftist newspapers in Europe. He's the first in print every time we screw something up and the first to write up the latest propaganda garbage that comes down from Hanoi. We've had our eyes on that bastard for a long time, but we've never been able to catch him at anything we could deport him for."

"What do you think he's got to do with this?"

"Obviously he's one of Tran's contacts, and I'll bet he's also connected to the Frenchman."

Santelli thought for a moment. "Since he's a journalist, do you think there's any chance he knows Laura?"

"That's an idea." Clifford frowned in concentration. "Who did you say she worked for?"

"UPI, I think."

"Good," Clifford said, reaching for the phone. "I've got a contact there and maybe he can help."

Santelli stood by while Clifford had a long conversation with the person on the other end of the line. When he hung up the phone, he was smiling.

"Bingo," he said gleefully. "We've got it. According to her desk calendar, she had an appointment with a 'Simon' at the Caravelle yesterday."

"I think we need to have a little talk with this guy," Santelli said with a big grin.

"You've got it."

WHEN SIMON HARRISON answered the knock at his door, he found himself staring down the muzzle of a large-caliber handgun. He was not a connoisseur of firearms, but he knew when he had a problem. Holding his hands in plain sight, he backed away from the door.

Two men in civilian clothes slipped into the room and closed the door behind them. "Simon Harrison?" the man with the gun asked.

"Yes," the reporter answered.

"I understand that you met with a Miss Laura Winthrop of United Press International at the Caravelle Hotel yesterday," Santelli said bluntly.

Harrison's mind raced, but he managed to look surprised. "Why, no. I haven't seen Laura in ages. Let me see, how long has it—"

Santelli's leg snapped out in a high kick, and the tip of his jungle boot caught the reporter directly between the legs. Harrison dropped to his knees, his hands cupped over his crotch and his mouth open in a soundless scream at the unbearable pain.

Santelli knelt down beside the reporter and, grabbing his hair, twisted his head around to face him. "I don't know how much you know about the States, scumbag, but my name's Jack Santelli of the New York Santellis. If you were from the Bronx, you'd know better than to try to screw around with me. I asked you a question and I damned well want a fucking answer."

Santelli smiled menacingly as he pulled Harrison up to his feet again. "Your future sex life depends on that answer, by the way. If I don't like what I hear, you're going to find your balls hanging out of your fuckin' ears. That's after, of course, I've stuffed your dick up your fat British ass."

"Okay, okay," Harrison gasped as soon as he could speak. "Yes, I saw Laura Winthrop. We had lunch at the Caravelle recently."

"What did you talk about?" Santelli asked.

Harrison tried a disarming smile. "Oh, we talked about her career and..."

Santelli's knee delivered a blow with stunning force. This time Harrison screamed as he fell to the floor. Santelli dropped to his side again and drilled the muzzle of the 9 mm pistol right between Harrison's eyes as the reporter fought for breath.

"You lied to me," Santelli said softly, "and I don't like that. If you lie to me one more time, you're going to wish that your father had cut your mother's throat the day he met the bitch."

It was quite some time before Harrison could speak again, and when he did, he couldn't get the words out fast enough. "The Frenchman." He spit the words out between gasps. "She wanted to know if I knew anything about a man called the Frenchman."

"What did you tell her?"

"I told her that I would try to find out who he was."

"Why would you tell her something like that?"

Harrison hesitated for a moment before answering. "I work for him."

Clifford took over the questioning now. "Who is he?"

"His name is Lucian de Champ."

Santelli and Clifford locked eyes over Harrison's head. Tran had called out for a Lucian in French and had called him his brother. Considering how many of the colonial French had taken Vietnamese mistresses, it could be true. If it was, it would explain why the Frenchman had come out from behind his well-established cover and had gone to these lengths to try to free a Vietnamese pimp and pornographer.

"Back to Laura," Santelli said abruptly. "You set her up to be kidnapped, right?"

Harrison nodded. "Yes."

"Where is she now?"

When Harrison hesitated again, Santelli pulled up his right pant leg, revealing a fighting knife in a sheath tied to the top of his jungle boot.

One look at the knife was enough to get past Harrison's mental block. "She's being held at the de Champ villa on the edge of a rubber plantation outside of Mimot, Cambodia."

"So far so good," Santelli said. "Now, tell me about Mike Reese, Captain Mike Reese."

"He's been taken to the same place," Harrison choked out. "He should arrive there this afternoon."

"Why is the Frenchman holding them hostage?"

"You are holding a man named Do Pham Tran, and Tran is his half brother."

Finally the last piece of the puzzle had clicked into place and was confirmed.

"They have the same father, right?" Clifford asked, and Harrison nodded.

"One last thing," Clifford said. "I want the names of all of the Frenchman's contacts."

"I don't know who..." Harrison started to say, but he stopped and swallowed hard when he saw Santelli polish the tip of his right jungle boot against the back of his left pant leg. "I will make a list of everyone I know."

Clifford escorted the reporter to his desk and, after checking to make sure that there were no weapons hidden in the desk drawers, handed him a yellow pad and a ballpoint pen. The reporter sat down and quickly wrote down several Vietnamese names and telephone numbers. When he was done, he handed the list to Clifford.

The CIA man studied the list before folding it and stuffing it into his shirt pocket.

"What do you want me to do with him?" Santelli asked as if Harrison wasn't sitting right there.

Clifford thought for a moment. Not only was Harrison a foreign national, but he was also a fairly prominent international journalist. If he were taken into custody, there would certainly be some serious political repercussions, and Clifford couldn't afford that. The Frenchman Project didn't need any more official notice: it was already in enough trouble as it was. He could have Santelli dispose of him, but that, too, presented problems. It was better if the reporter left the scene alive and well.

"Convince him to leave town."

Santelli looked at the CIA man. "Why not just drop him in the river?"

"I'd love to, but it'd cause us too many problems. Just see that he gets the hell out of here. Today."

"You are going to leave Vietnam," Santelli said softly as he bent over to speak in the reporter's ear. "No, better than that, you are going to leave Southeast Asia entirely. You have suddenly come down with an incurable disease and have to go back to England for emergency medical treatment. Something about the climate here really disagrees with you, and if you ever return for any reason, you're going to die a horrible death. You got that?"

The reporter nodded numbly.

"Oh," Santelli added, nudging the muzzle of his Hi-Power under the reporter's chin, "I almost forgot. Your incurable disease is called a 9 mm slug behind the ear. If you're still in town by sundown, your disease is going to suddenly strike you down."

Harrison was still sitting in the chair when the two Americans let themselves out of the apartment.

"I didn't know that you were connected with the mob," Clifford said once they were back on the street outside Harrison's apartment building.

Santelli grinned. "I'm not, but there's no way that sorry bastard could have known that. That's one of the advantages of having an Italian name."

"You've been watching too many gangster movies."

"No," Santelli said seriously, "I just grew up in an interesting neighborhood."

Clifford shook his head. "Jesus."

HARRISON PAINFULLY dragged himself to his feet and glanced at his watch. If he hurried, he could just make the last Air Vietnam flight of the day to Bangkok, Thailand, and go from there to India. Once he was in India, it would be easy for him to get a flight back to London.

His eyes wandered aimlessly around his richly furnished apartment. He had spent a fortune over the years filling the place with fine French antiques and priceless Oriental art, but there was no time to pack anything more than a few changes of clothes and some personal effects. He would have to write one of his friends later and ask him to dispose of the apartment and his belongings. He would be certain to lose most of that fortune he had spent on the place, but at least he would still be alive.

He briefly thought of trying to get a message to the Frenchman but quickly discarded that idea. Whoever that Santelli really was, Harrison had no doubt that he was having him watched. He also had no doubt that Santelli would kill him unless he did exactly what he'd been told. Also, contacting de Champ would only let the Frenchman know that he had talked, and that would definitely cost him his life.

At least the American had given him a way to escape death, but only if the Frenchman died. De Champ's criminal contacts reached all the way into Europe, and the only hope Harrison had to stay alive was if the Americans killed him.

Simon Harrison was many things, but brave or self-sacrificing was not one of them. Grabbing a small suitcase from the closet, he frantically started stuffing clothes into it.

13

August 18, Cholon

Back at the safehouse, Santelli started to put the mission together as fast as he could. The longer Reese was in the Frenchman's hands, the greater the chance that he would be killed or injured. Santelli wasn't half so worried about Laura's safety, though, as he was about his captain's. As far as he was concerned, he hadn't really cared much for the blond reporter from the minute he had met her. She was a little too WASPish for Santelli's Italian tastes, and he was also put off by something cold and ambitious about her. Had she been a long black-haired Mediterranean beauty with big eyes, he might have been a little more sympathetic, but her Scandinavian type beauty seemed lacking in human warmth.

Reese, on the other hand, was one of the best men he had ever worked with, in or out of the Army. He thought his CO's mind was more than a little scrambled for having gotten so involved with Laura. But other than that, Santelli respected him and would do everything he could to get him out of this. He would probably privately kick his ass up between his ears when this was all over, but that would be later. Right now he had to concentrate on rescue efforts.

The first thing Santelli did was to place a land-line call to CCC in Kontum to talk to Major Snow. Though still recovering from the wound he had suffered in the assassination attempt, the Hungarian operations officer was back hard at work. And this was exactly the kind of operation he specialized in: totally covert, very risky and aimed at someone who badly needed to be taken out.

Also, Snow had a personal stake in this mission. As a member of SOG's "Get the Frenchman" committee, he knew that if de Champ wasn't stopped cold, there was a good chance the next attempt on his life wouldn't fail. Also, he owed Reese a big one. Like Santelli, he couldn't believe that Reese had let himself get in that deep over a woman. But when he remembered his wife and child, who had died in Budapest during the Hungarian Revolution, he was more disposed to cut Reese a little slack on that issue. The important thing now was to get him back to Vietnam in one piece. He'd eat his ass out about it later.

After making some preliminary plans, Snow assured Santelli that Kowalski, Wilson, Hotchkiss and the two Nungs from A-410 could be freed up for the rescue attempt. Given the situation, it was best to keep it within the family, and the men would be delivered to Tan Son Nhut as fast as the chopper could pick them up from the Dak Sang camp and fly them to a waiting plane at Kontum. Snow would also see to it that the necessary mission equipment was loaded onto the plane.

"Okay," Santelli said, putting the phone back down. "Major Snow's got something going for us here."

"What's that?"

"The major's sending five of my people from the A-team and we're going to do a HALO jump into Cambodia."

"What the fuck's a HALO?"

Santelli grinned. "High-Altitude, Low-Opening parachute jump. We exit the aircraft at about 15-16 thousand feet, free-fall most of the way and then pop the chutes a thousand feet off the ground. That way, nobody sees the aircraft fly over, and if we're lucky, no one sees us, either."

"Then what are you going to do?"

"That's the easy part." Santelli grinned. "Once we're on the ground, we're going to knock over de Champ's villa and get the captain back."

"Is that going to be enough people to do the job?"

"I plan to ask our sniper if he wants to go along with us. We can use his long-range shooting on this one, too."

Santelli and Clifford found the Indian sniper in the basement pulling maintenance on some of the weapons. Since the raid on Tran's place, he'd had little to do, but he was hanging around because he knew that it wasn't over yet. If he was reading this situation right, there'd be more opportunities for him to pop caps on the bad guys.

"We're going into Cambodia to get Captain Reese back," Santelli told him. "You want to go along?"

"Sure thing, sir."

"You ever made a parachute jump?"

The Indian sniper shook his head. "I was in too big a hurry to get over here," he said. "I didn't have time to go through jump school."

"You want to try it anyway?"

Chief grinned. "Sure, LT, why not. If the fucking thing doesn't work, I can always take it back, right?"

Santelli grinned at the old joke. "Right. Return it and get your money back."

"I want in on this, too," Clifford butted into the conversation. "I'll make the jump with you."

Santelli shook his head. "Sorry. One cherry jumper on a HALO mission is one too many. It's just too dangerous. Plus—" he held up his hand to keep Clifford from replying before he was finished "—we'll need someone back here to coordinate this thing. When we get them back, we're going to need to get the hell outta there A-fucking-SAP, and we can't have any last-minute fuckups. We'll need you to be on top of this every second."

Even though Clifford wanted to be in on the kill, he recognized the wisdom of Santelli's words and was forced to agree. "Okay, just as long as you make sure you waste the Frenchman for me."

"We'll get him if we can," Santelli said, locking eyes with the CIA agent. "But our primary mission is to free Reese and Laura, and I won't jeopardize that just to kill this guy for you. Now that you know where he is, though, as soon as Reese is outta there, you can send an Arc Light strike in on his ass for all I care."

"Just make sure that you at least try to get him, okay?" Clifford growled.

"We'll try," Santelli said sincerely. "But that's all I can promise right now."

"I'll settle for that."

LAURA'S JOURNEY seemed to be taking hours, but blindfolded as she was, she had no idea how long it had actually been. It had gotten warmer, however, so she knew that the sun had come up again. At first the Land Rover had taken badly rutted back roads, but later the ride had smoothed out as if they were traveling on a major highway. The driver had stopped several times, and she had heard low voices speaking Vietnamese, but since she didn't understand the language, she had no idea what they were saying.

She was getting angry and badly needed to relieve her bladder when the truck slowed and came to a complete stop. The driver came back, untied her and helped her down to the ground. When her blindfold was removed, she saw that she was inside the walled compound of a large French colonial villa situated in a small valley surrounded by gently rolling hills covered with trees planted in neat rows.

As she stood, rubbing her wrists, a tall, older Caucasian man walked down the front steps of the villa toward her. "Welcome to Château de Champ, Miss Winthrop," the man said, extending his hand. "I am Lucian de Champ and I will be your host for the next few days."

Stunned by her reception, Laura automatically took his hand. "Where am I?" she asked.

De Champ smiled. "You are a little south of Mimot, Cambodia." His hand swept to indicate the orderly ranks of trees on the surrounding hills. "These are my family's rubber plantations."

"You're the man they call the Frenchman, aren't you?" she asked, remembering why she was there.

The welcoming smile did not leave de Champ's face. "Yes," he said. "I believe that some of you Americans do call me that. Considering my nationality, however, it is not an overly imaginative title for me."

"Am I your prisoner, then?"

De Champ paused for a moment. "No," he said. "I want you to think of yourself as my guest. It has been a long time since I have had guests. Particularly one as lovely as you."

Laura brushed aside his attempt at gallantry. "But when can I go back to Saigon?"

"That may take a while, my dear," he said, and took her arm. "But come inside and we will talk about your visit."

Laura let de Champ lead her into the villa and on into a beautiful sitting room furnished in French style. He clapped his hands, and a servant immediately appeared. "May I offer you some iced tea?"

"Yes, please," she answered, "but I need to use the bathroom first."

"Of course," he said. "I should have thought of that...it has been a long trip for you. This way, please." De Champ led her to a door off the sitting room and waited outside for her.

Inside, Laura tried to collect her thoughts as she used the facilities, then splashed water from the basin onto her face and hands. She was relieved that de Champ had turned out to be such a charming man, but after having spent the night in the truck, she was still frightened. Hurriedly she patted her face dry and left the bathroom, not wanting de Champ to think that she was stalling.

"I understand that you work for the United Press agency," de Champ said after she was seated on the couch, a glass of freshly made iced tea in her hand.

Laura nodded.

"How did you decide that you wanted to do a story on me?" he asked.

"Ah . . . I heard your nickname," Laura lied badly, "and some stories about you . . . and I decided that I wanted to know who you really were. I talked to Simon, Simon Harrison, about you and he said he'd try to help me. I . . . I didn't know that he knew you."

"Oh yes," De Champ replied. "Mr. Harrison and I are old friends. We have served the cause together for many years now."

"You are a Communist, then?"

"Some people would call me that," de Champ admitted, a note of indignation in his voice. "But I think that is a limited term. I prefer to think of myself as a fighter for the international brotherhood of man. Surely you are familiar with the works of Marx and Lenin, but maybe as an American you do not understand the true plight of the masses in the less-developed countries, like Vietnam and Cambodia.''

''I've seen quite a bit of Vietnam,'' she defended herself, ''and I know that there are lots of social problems in this part of the world. But I don't think that communism is the answer for these people. Just look at the problems they have in Red China.''

''We can discuss this at greater length later,'' de Champ said. ''Now perhaps I should show you to your quarters. I'm sure that you are tired after your long journey.''

''Thank you.''

''Oh,'' de Champ added with a smile, ''I almost forgot. Your friend, Captain Mike Reese, is on his way here to see you. He gave himself up to guarantee your safety and he will join you here later this afternoon.''

Rather than being cheered by the news, Laura felt even more depressed, feeling she had endangered Mike, as well.

De Champ led her along a hall to steps going down into a basement. The subterranean level didn't look much like a place for a guest room, but she followed the Frenchman until he stopped at a door. Two men in black pajama uniforms carrying AKs were waiting at the door, and Laura's heart sank when one of them opened the door. The room inside was a cell barely two by three meters, with bars over the single window, a cot and a bucket.

''But you said I was your guest!''

''You are, my dear,'' de Champ said, motioning for her to enter. ''But I am afraid that I am a little short of more-suitable accommodations for you. So for the moment this will have to do."

"You lied to me, you bastard!"

De Champ smiled without warmth. "Simon was wrong about you, Miss Winthrop. Apparently you are somewhat more intelligent than you appear most of the time."

Laura had no answer to that as she walked into the cell and heard the door lock behind her.

IT WAS LATE AFTERNOON by the time the Special Forces men from A-410 at Dak Sang showed up at the Tan Son Nhut air base. Santelli and Clifford were on hand to meet them at the chopper pad with a three-quarter-ton truck. Along with the men, the CCC chopper was loaded with the bags containing the HALO jump equipment.

Clifford had met all of the Americans before on an earlier operation, but none of them seemed overwhelmed at seeing him again. The CIA man had come to expect that kind of treatment from the Special Forces, however, and wasn't surprised. Had they been glad to see him, he would have been instantly suspicious.

Little was said as the equipment was loaded into the truck, and the five men climbed into the back for the ride to the safehouse.

Silk Wilson looked out the back of the truck as it drove through downtown Saigon. "Man, I sure hope the LT turns us loose for a night or two here before we go back. It's been a long time since I've had any big-city boom-boom.''

"Shit, man," Kowalski said. "Boom-boom is boom-boom. It ain't any better here than it is back in Kontum, take my word for it. I've been laid here before, and it just wasn't that great."

The black medic turned to the Alabama-born Kowalski. "That's because you're a pecker-wood, 'Bama redneck, Ski," he said, grinning widely. "And you don't know how to find the good stuff. Any big-city man knows he can find himself some real hot action in a place like this."

Hotchkiss snorted. "The only thing you're going to find here, Silk, is a raging case of clap. At least you *Bac Sis* keep the girls back at Kontum halfway clean. No one's checking the whores here. You catch the clap here, and the old man will put you up on charges of damaging government equipment."

Wilson laughed at the old joke, but was still determined to get his night on the town before he had to go back to the remote border camp he called home. It had been a long time since he had seen the bright lights of a real city.

The two Nungs were even more fascinated with the prospects of a little R and R in Saigon than Wilson was. Neither one of them had ever been to the capital city before. The interpreter known as Cowboy was particularly fascinated by the idea. "Hey, *Trung Si* Ski," he said. "Maybe I go tee-tee AWOL before we go back to Dak Sang, okay?"

"You go AWOL on me, you little shit," Kowalski growled, "and I'll sic the White Mice on your young ass. Then I'll let them keep you in the monkey house for a month before seeing they draft you into the fuckin' ARVN."

Cowboy was shocked to think that Kowalski would think of turning him over to the Vietnamese National Police, the White Mice, even as a joke. And the threat of being drafted into the Vietnamese army was worse than a bad joke. It would be almost a guaranteed death sentence for him, and Ski knew that. "Hey, *Trung Si,*" he said indignantly. "That not very funny. You be nice!"

"You just keep your ass outta trouble, then, Cowboy, or I'll do it to you for sure."

While Kowalski wasn't enthusiastic about Saigon, he was even less pleased about why he was in town. Major Snow had given them a partial briefing at Kontum before they flew out, and while he didn't know all the details of the plan, he knew enough to be scared shitless. As the A-410's Intelligence specialist, he knew better than to go into that particular part of Cambodia with anything less than a full division at his back and a fleet of B-52s flying air support.

No matter what Santelli was going to tell them at the final briefing, he knew this one was going to be a bastard.

14

August 18, Mimot, Cambodia

When Reese's blindfold was removed at the end of his long journey, he was looking out onto the front yard of a large French-colonial-style villa. Extensive rubber plantations covered the surrounding low, red hills as far as he could see, and he knew instantly that he was in Cambodia, probably somewhere north of the Parrot's Beak area. All the rubber plantations this large in Vietnam had been cut down or bombed out a long time ago.

Stepping out of the Citroën, Reese saw a tall Caucasian man approach the car, escorted by two NVA carrying AKs. It had to be the elusive Frenchman, but Reese couldn't see anything extraordinary about him. He had almost expected the legendary master spy to be something special, but this man was just another typical middle-aged Frenchman. He was tall and slender with a neatly combed shock of light brown hair, and he was dressed in the colonial plantation owner's uniform of light linen slacks and a white shirt open at the neck.

"I am Lucian de Champ," the man said, and extended his hand. "I think you know me by the rather unimaginative title of 'the Frenchman.' And you, of course, are Captain Michael Reese of the American Special Forces.''

Reese was surprised and took his hand but didn't say that he was pleased to meet him. The only way that would have been true would be if he had met the Frenchman over the sights of an M-16.

There was an awkward pause as Reese remained silent, waiting for the Frenchman's next move. "Come with me, please," de Champ finally said.

Two guards fell in beside him as de Champ led Reese into the villa and along a long hall leading to steps down into a basement. "Miss Winthrop is waiting for you," he said. "The guards will take you to her."

Reese followed them down the steps without saying a word.

LAURA LOOKED UP when she heard footsteps approaching the door to her cell. Except for guards who had brought her meals, she had been left completely alone since arriving at de Champ's villa. It was not mealtime, so she stiffened, preparing herself for whatever was coming. The door slowly opened, and Reese appeared with two of the North Vietnamese guards standing behind him. He stepped inside, and the guards locked the door behind him.

She rushed to him. "Mike! What are you doing here?"

He stepped back from her. "I could almost ask you the same thing."

As happy as she was to see him, she was stunned by the tone of his voice and the cold look he gave her. A hundred things went through her mind.... Did he know what she had been working on when she had been taken captive, and did he know why she had been working on it?

"What do you mean?"

"You went through my briefcase the night I came back from the field, didn't you?"

She hesitated for a moment. "Mike, I'm sorry, I didn't know. I knew that you were working on another secret SOG assignment and I just got curious."

"You wanted your 'big story,' right?"

Laura had the decency to look ashamed. "I read the file on de Champ and when I saw the words 'terminate with extreme prejudice,' I thought it would be a good story."

Reese slowly shook his head. Of all of the stupid, dumb-ass things he had ever heard of, this had to be the all-time world champion. Those four words made brave men quake in their boots, but she had thought they were only an invitation to journalistic glory. She had not understood that they were really an invitation to a lonely death and an unmarked grave far from home.

"You realize, of course, that de Champ's going to kill both of us, don't you?" Reese's voice was harsh as he explained the reality of their situation. "We're supposed to be exchanged for a prisoner Clifford is holding back in Saigon, but there's no fucking way he can turn us loose. We know too much about him now.''

Laura recoiled as though she had been slapped. She had spent her time worrying about being tortured or raped and hadn't given much coherent thought to the reality of her situation. She slowly sat down on the edge of the narrow cot and put her face in her hands. "Oh God, Mike. I'm so sorry. I didn't realize."

"You do now."

Laura started to weep silently, her shoulders shaking, but Reese made no move to comfort her. He had spotted the miniature microphones in the corners of the ceiling and knew that de Champ was listening in on their little drama. As far as he was concerned, he wanted the Frenchman to know that he knew the score, but he also wanted him to wonder why he had given himself up if it wasn't to protect Laura. He wanted de Champ to think that he had a plan.

Actually Reese didn't have the slightest idea how the hell he was going to get out of this one alive, much less get Laura out with him. The only thing he thought he might be able to do was buy them some time. He knew that Santelli would force Clifford into making a rescue attempt, and he was counting on Santelli to pull it off somehow. Until then, though, he had to keep both of them alive.

As DE CHAMP LISTENED to his two American prisoners talk, a frown formed on his face. So far, the conversation was not going as he would have expected it to go. It did not sound like a reunion of lovers terrified for each other's safety. From the information he had, he was certain that they had been sleeping together, and Reese's giving himself up in hopes of saving her confirmed that. But he didn't sound as though he was very much in love with her right now. In fact, it sounded as if he was more than thoroughly disgusted with her.

The frown deepened on the Frenchman's face. Maybe he had overestimated Reese's relationship with the girl; maybe the Special Forces officer had given himself up for another reason. Perhaps he had some vain hope that he would be able to free her and escape. If that was the case, however, de Champ had bad news for him. No one had ever gotten away from his cells in the basement of the de Champ villa.

"Tape everything they say," he said in French to his radioman. "I want to listen to it later."

"Yes, Comrade de Champ."

Outside the radio room, de Champ sent a servant to get the captain of his security force. Even though he ran his operation from deep inside neutral Cambodia, he knew he was a prime target for the American CIA and guarded his villa well. The main-force Vietcong headquarters in his district provided him with a dozen men and a nearby Vietcong main-force company was on call if he should need them. Perhaps it would be a wise move to reinforce his security force until he was finished with Reese.

WITH LAURA CRYING to herself, there was little else for him to say, so Reese slipped his boots off to make himself more comfortable. Taking the extra blanket from the end of Laura's cot, he folded it up into a pillow and lay down on the concrete floor. The first thing he wanted to do was to get some rest while he still had the chance. Within minutes he was fast asleep.

When Laura saw that Reese had gone to sleep, at first she couldn't believe her eyes, then she got flaming mad. Goddamn him! Who the hell did he think he was to come in here and treat her this way? She was crying because she was afraid that they were both going to die, and all he could do was to ignore her and lie down on the hard floor to take a nap. She was of half a mind to walk over and kick him in the ribs, but she was suddenly afraid of him.

Just as when she had read the CIA termination order, she felt a shiver pass through her. What kind of man was this Mike Reese, anyway? She had thought that she knew him well, but she now realized that she really didn't know him at all. From the very beginning, this whole nightmare had revealed aspects of him that she had not seen before. For one, he was obviously an assassin...why else would he be working for the CIA on an assignment to kill de Champ?

But more importantly, today she had seen an icy coldness instead of the love and warmth she had come to expect from him. From the way he had greeted her and the things he had said, she seriously doubted that he cared for her at all. His earlier behavior had obviously only been an act to get her into bed, and that angered her. It made her so mad that it never crossed her mind to ask herself why he had allowed himself to be captured and brought to Cambodia if he didn't really care for her.

Had she been a little less distraught and thinking more clearly, Laura might have realized that he was putting on an act for de Champ's benefit. But then, had she been thinking more clearly, neither one of them would have been in this situation in the first place.

She lay down on her cot, but unlike Reese, she tossed restlessly and was not able to go to sleep. Reese's soft snoring did nothing to improve her mood, either. Instead of counting sheep, she counted new names to call Reese as soon as he woke up.

IN THE BASEMENT of the Cholon safehouse, Santelli watched as Chief, Kowalski, Hotchkiss, Wilson and the two Nungs prepared for the mission. He was confident that he had the right team assembled for this operation.

Alabama-born SF Sergeant Gil Kowalski was one of the best Intelligence men he had ever met, as well as being a tiger in the field. SFC Vic Hotchkiss was his small-arms expert and could serve as Chief's spotter and backup shooter in case anything happened to the Indian sniper. Chicago-born Staff Sergeant Silk Wilson was more than just a good combat medic because he had taken the street-fighting skills he had learned in his hometown and had honed them to a fine edge in the bush.

Santelli would have preferred to have another interpreter instead of Cowboy, since the young Nung had a habit of not taking things seriously enough at times. But Cowboy was the only one in the Dak Sang camp who had a good working knowledge of several dialects of Cambodian, as well as English. Ninh, the other Nung, was a good tracker, and he had enough English to communicate well with the team.

Except for Chief, all the men were airborn qualified, and Santelli put Silk Wilson to work teaching the Indian sniper the rudiments of parachute jumping, particularly those things that he would need to know to survive the HALO jump. Wilson had more time in a parachute harness than anyone else in the team and usually served as their jumpmaster when they made their drops.

While his teammates went over their weapons and gear, Wilson pulled Chief aside. "Free-falling," he told the sniper, "is easy just as long as you remember a few things. First and foremost, you have to get into the right free-fall position, facedown. You remember the old Superman movies?"

Chief nodded.

"Well, that's the position you've got to be in. Arms and legs spread out like a starfish, and you've got to be facedown. If you roll over onto your back, you'll ball up and fall too fast. The way to get into the right position is to exit the aircraft properly. To do that, however, takes a pair of brass balls."

The Indian grinned.

"Rather than jump feet first like you would for a static-line jump," Wilson continued, "you have to throw yourself out of the plane like you're throwing yourself on some whore's bed. Facedown, arms and legs out and go for it." The medic grinned. "You know the position."

Chief grinned even wider.

"In just a few seconds you'll be falling at what we call terminal velocity, a little over a hundred and twenty miles per hour, but you won't notice it. With the helmet, mask and goggles blocking the wind, all you'll see is the ground coming closer to you."

"Now, you can steer yourself while you're falling. Watch the rest of the guys and try to stay up with them. If you want to turn right, pull your left arm in. To go left, use the right arm. To go faster, tuck your arms in closer to your sides. To slow down, hold them out. You got that?"

The sniper was listening intently, absorbing every word, and he nodded enthusiastically.

"Your chute pack has an altimeter and an automatic release, but you can't count on it working right. If you see the other guys suddenly disappear upward, it means that their chutes have popped and you've fallen past them. If that happens, you've got to pull your manual release yourself. And pull it fast 'cause you'll only have a few seconds left before you hit the ground."

Wilson stopped to take a deep breath, then went on again. "If you've kept up with the rest of us," Wilson continued, "you'll be lined up okay for the drop zone. But if you've drifted away, to control your chute you want your hands up on the risers. They're the straps on the harness to go up past your shoulders. Pull down on the right side to correct to the right, left side to go left.''

"And then comes the only real hard part of this whole exercise, the landing. If you don't hit just right, you're going to break something for sure. If that happens on this mission, we're going to have to leave you behind. So, when you hit, you have to go into what's known in the trade as a PLF, a Parachute Landing Fall.''

Wilson led the sniper over to the weapons-cleaning table. "Hop up,'' he said, and Chief did as he was told.

"Okay, now stand on the edge with your knees flexed and your arms up as if you're holding on to the chute risers. Holding that position, I want you to jump down. And when you hit, take up the shock with your legs and roll over onto your right side. Let yourself fall, don't try to stay on your feet. Go!''

Chief assumed the strange position and jumped. Following Wilson's instruction, he let his legs take up the shock and went down on his right side.

"Try it a few times,'' Wilson said. "But keep your arms up this time.''

Santelli came up and pulled Wilson aside. "How's he doing?''

The medic glanced over to where Chief was doing practice PLFs off the top of the table. "I'd like to have a day with him in a decent training facility,'' he said. "But I think he'll do okay.''

"You want to go down holding his hands?" Santelli asked, referring to free-fall jumpers linking hands to stay together as they fell.

Wilson shook his head. "Not on the first jump, LT," he said. "If he gets in trouble during the free-fall, I'll try to get him turned around, but I don't want to link up with him. If he freezes up, he might get me all fucked up, too, and then you'd lose both of us."

"You've got a point there," Santelli agreed. "I guess we'll just have to let him go it on his own. Make sure, though, that you teach him everything you can. He's not SOG—hell, he isn't even SF, so if we lose him on this, I'll have a hell of a lot of explaining to do."

"I'll do the best I can, LT."

As soon as all the gear was ready, Santelli had everyone call it quits for the night. Since they were leaving so early in the morning, he was having them all sleep in the safehouse. Wilson and Cowboy wanted to go out for a quick drink, but the lieutenant quickly quashed that idea. He knew what they were really after, and this mission was ample indication of what could happen when men were led around by their urges. He was not going to let them out of his sight for an instant until they were on the ground in Cambodia.

15

August 19, High over Cambodia

The battered Fairchild C-123 Provider cargo plane whined, wheezed, shook and rattled as it reached its cruising altitude of sixteen thousand feet. Unlike the unmarked Loach that had transported Reese's team on the abortive mission to the Straight Edge Woods, this plane was bare aluminum and bore the words Air America, a prominent American flag and a serial number on its tall tail fin.

Air America was the air transport arm of the CIA and, while it was supposed to be a secret, it was the poorest kept secret in all of Southeast Asia. Everyone from the Saigon shoeshine boys on up knew who was actually running the unscheduled airline. Besides flying pigs and rice to remote mountaintop Laotian outposts, Air America also occasionally carried classified cargo for the CIA and SOG.

The seven men wearing HALO rigs in the back this time were considered to be classified cargo. The fact that they were going to deliver this cargo from sixteen thousand feet did not matter to the Air America pilots flying the Provider. They were used to unusual cargo-delivery instructions.

As soon as today's cargo exited the ship, the Provider would continue on to Laos, where it would land and take on another strange cargo load. It could even be a water buffalo or neatly wrapped ten-kilo blocks of raw opium. The pilots could not have cared less what was put into their planes. All that mattered to them was that they got it to where it was supposed to go more or less on time.

In the back of the Provider, Santelli and his six HALO jumpers got ready for their drop. Along with their backpack parachutes, the men had their loaded jungle rucks, ammunition and weapons strapped to their bodies and were wearing oxygen masks hanging around their necks. With a whine from electric motors, the Provider's rear ramp door slowly lowered into the open position, and a red light came on next to it.

Santelli stood and yelled over the roar of the engines, instructing the team to line up on the ramp. As a cherry jumper, Chief was spotted to be the third man out the door in case someone needed to push him out. As soon as the men were in position, Santelli pulled his oxygen mask up over his mouth, and everyone else did the same. Next the men paired off and checked each other's jump gear. Since Chief didn't know what to check, Wilson gave him his last check and patted him on the back to let him know that everything was secure.

When the green light came on, Santelli stepped out into space, assumed a spread-eagle, free-fall position and started plunging toward earth. Looking back, he saw the rest of the team stacked up above him. Everyone, including the sniper, looked to be in a good free-fall position. One of the men was positioned close to Chief's right side, and he knew that Wilson was keeping an eye on the sniper.

Santelli aimed himself for the drop zone below, a small cleared field surrounded by patches of woods. At two thousand feet above the ground, he reached his right hand over to his chest and grasped the manual-release D ring firmly. If the parachute failed to deploy at the right altitude, he had only a split second to pop it manually before he made a big, wet hole in the red Cambodian earth.

At exactly one thousand feet, the altimeter triggered the backpack parachute. The small pilot parachute popped out, snapped open and pulled the main canopy out of the pack. Santelli's plunging descent was brought to an abrupt halt that threatened to drive his testicles up into his groin. That was the only thing he hated about HALO jumps. He could never pull the crotch straps tight enough.

After quickly checking his own risers and canopy, he looked to see if the rest of the men had good parachute deployment. One of the Nungs seemed to be having trouble with a partially opened canopy, but everyone else looked good. The Nung was light enough that he should make it down okay even with a partial deployment.

The ground approached rapidly, and bending his knees, Santelli took up the landing shock with a controlled fall and rolled over onto his right side in a classic PLF. Jumping to his feet, he quickly hauled in on the risers to collapse the parachute canopy before he was dragged across the open field. As soon as his chute was spilled, he triggered the harness release and quickly shrugged out of the gear.

His eyes sweeping the nearby woods, he quickly unclipped his rucksack and freed his weapons. Pulling back on the charging handle of his CAR-15, he chambered a round before shouldering his ruck. Now he was ready, and the first thing he did was to check on his cherry jumper.

The sniper was gathering his parachute when Santelli walked up to him. "Man, what a ride!" he said enthusiastically, his eyes glittering from the adrenaline rush. He reached down and dusted the red Cambodian dirt from the knees of his tiger-suit pants.

Santelli grinned. "I thought you'd like it."

"When do I get to do it again?"

"You're the only guy I know who's ever done a HALO for his first jump," Santelli said. "And you're lucky to be alive, so don't press your luck."

"I'm going to airborne school for sure when I rotate," Chief promised. "This shit's fun!"

Santelli grinned. "I've created another jumpin' junkie."

By now everyone was suited up and they dragged their parachutes and rigging to the edge of the tree line and stuffed them out of sight under the brush. As soon as the DZ had been cleared, the team established a defensive perimeter in the wood line. Inside the perimeter, the first thing Santelli did was to break out his map and compass to make sure that they had landed on the proper drop zone. More than one airborne operation had gone tits up because the paratroopers had not been dropped in the right place. Taking a compass reading to the two mountain peaks in the distance and running a back azimuth on the map, he found that they had been delivered to the right spot.

"Okay," he said, folding the map so that only their planned route to the villa was showing. "We're here and we need to go there. We're going to have to be careful because it's pretty open country, and Major Snow says that this place is crawling with hard-hat NVA. Our assembly area is less than a hour from the de Champ villa. Once there, we'll check out the compound and plan our assault after dark. If possible, we'll try to kill the Frenchman, but our priority is to rescue the captain and the girl. When we've freed them, we'll pull back and beat feet for the PZ, where we'll be extracted by an Air America chopper."

It wasn't a fancy plan, and there were holes in it a mile wide, but it was all he had been able to come up with on such short notice. He would have liked to have a diversion or two laid on, something like an Arc Light strike. But, as with the Straight Edge Woods mission, playing with the CIA meant playing by their rules and that meant no help.

"Any questions at this point?"

There were none. On a mission like this, it either worked or they all died.

"If we run into anything we can't handle and have to pull back, this will be our rendezvous point." He folded the map and put it in his side pants pocket. "Okay, let's get it."

SHORTLY AFTER a meager breakfast had been delivered to their cell, Reese heard the footsteps of two men approaching the door.

"What is it?" Laura asked as he slipped his boots on and stood.

Reese managed a thin smile. "De Champ wants to talk to me."

"How do you know that?"

"That's just the way these things work," he said. "I'm a danger to him, and he wants to know what we've learned about him."

When the door opened, one of the Vietnamese guards held an AK on him while the other one said, "You. Come."

The Vietnamese escorted Reese into a large study on the first floor of the house. De Champ was seated behind an ornately carved black teakwood desk. When Reese entered, one of the guards moved to the far side of the room so he could keep him covered. The Frenchman rose and motioned to a brocaded chair. "Captain Reese, please have a seat."

Reese sat down but didn't speak.

"Can I offer you a coffee with a spot of brandy?"

"Yes, please," Reese said. "That's rather civilized of you."

"There is no point in not being civilized," de Champ said, pouring a cup of coffee from the silver urn on his desk and adding it to a tray with a small snifter of brandy. "That is one of the biggest problems I have encountered in my various dealings with you Americans. You think that you have to hate your enemies and treat them barbarically. Even though you and I are at war, as it were, there is no need for me to treat you in an uncivilized manner."

De Champ handed the tray to Reese. "That is, just as long as you reciprocate."

"Which means that if I tell you what you want to know, you won't have it beaten out of me."

De Champ smiled. "You are obviously an intelligent man, Captain, and I think we will get along well. One thing, I admit, though, that puzzles me is why you allowed yourself to be captured this way. That does not speak much of your intelligence."

Reese shrugged and took a big swallow of the coffee. "Men often do unintelligent things for their women."

De Champ did not let Reese know that he was fully aware that the American had not shown any great love for his mistress so far. In fact, he had been quite harsh with her and had not even made love to her during the night. He had reviewed the tapes the first thing this morning and had been surprised to find that the microphones had not picked up the expected sounds of tearful lovers.

"That is so," he said after sipping his own brandy.

Reese didn't reply, but downed the rest of the coffee. He needed the caffeine to get his brain working. De Champ saw and refilled the cup.

"Now," de Champ said, "perhaps we should get down to business, as you Americans say. First of all, who are you working for?"

Reese knew better than to try the name-rank-and-service-number bit on this guy. If Clifford's assessment of the Frenchman's Intelligence network was correct, he already knew everything there was to know about him, including his shoe size and blood type. There was no point in giving de Champ an excuse to hammer the information out of him.

"I am assigned to Fifth Group, U.S. Special Forces, but I'm opcon to MACV-SOG."

"Opcon." De Champ frowned. "I do not understand what that means. It is sometimes difficult for me to keep up with the latest American slang."

"It means that I'm under their operational control," Reese explained. "I work for them."

"I see," the Frenchman replied. "And who exactly do you work for in SOG?"

"Dick Clifford of the operations section."

"The CIA agent?"

"Yes."

"You are an assassin, no?"

Reese shook his head. "No, I'm just a run-of-the-mill Special Forces officer."

"Then why are you involved with this affair?"

Reese locked eyes with the Frenchman and let his voice show a touch of anger. "You tried to have a friend of mine killed in Nha Trang, a Major Jan Snow."

"I see. You think that I ordered the assassination of your friend, so you joined the CIA effort to hunt me down."

"Something like that."

De Champ paused to pour another splash of brandy in his glass. "How American."

"It pissed me off." Reese held out his own brandy glass for a refill. "Jan's a good buddy of mine."

"You must have been the one at the restaurant with the major, then."

"Yeah," Reese admitted, "That was me."

"You proved to be very good that evening," de Champ said with grudging admiration. "I understand that you killed both of my men yourself."

Reese shrugged. "They really weren't all that good. You shouldn't have used them for a hit like that. They were way out of their league. You should have sent some pros after him like the ones you used for the Saigon hit on Major Johnson."

"Next time I will."

"There won't be a next time," Reese said. "Jan's on to you now, and you won't sneak up on him again."

De Champ didn't reply but changed the topic. "How did you and Clifford come to learn about Do Pham Tran?"

"That was easy." Reese smiled. "We caught one of his boys peddling dirty pictures to GIs and we traced them back to him. When we busted his joint, we found his wall safe full of that stuff."

"My brother is not a pornographer!" de Champ snapped.

"You could have fooled us," Reese replied, a little surprised by de Champ's response. But now he knew why the Frenchman had gone to such lengths to get the Vietnamese back. "He had hundreds of negatives showing American GIs screwing Dink whores. He must really get off on that sort of thing or something."

De Champ reined in his anger. "That is not important now. The important thing is freeing my brother from your CIA."

"Clifford will be glad to let you have him." Reese smiled. "He's of no further use to us now. We got everything we wanted from him without having to lay a hand on him."

"What do you mean?"

"What I mean is that he shot his mouth off as fast as he could, hoping to buy his way out of there with information."

"You are lying," de Champ said angrily. "Tran would have never talked."

Reese shrugged nonchalantly. "Suit yourself. But we've got your whole Saigon network wrapped up. Oh sure, we probably missed a few of the small fish, but we got all of the major players. Your little operation is *fini.*"

De Champ was silent for a moment. If what Reese said was even half-true, he was in great danger. Depending on what Tran had revealed to them, he might be forced to rebuild his entire operation. But as long as he had Reese and the woman in his custody, he had time to evaluate the damage instead of merely reacting.

"I will contact Clifford today to set up the exchange," de Champ promised. "Until then, you will rejoin Miss Winthrop."

Seeing that the interview was at an end, Reese got to his feet. "Oh," he said. "One more thing. When you talk to Dick Clifford, tell him that he'd better not fuck up the exchange and fail to get me out of here on time. I'll have his ass if he does."

The Frenchman looked at him coldly. "You will get out of here on time, Captain, I can promise you that."

Reese met his eyes. "Good. I'm counting on it."

16

August 19, Mimot, Cambodia

After ordering the Vietnamese guard to escort Reese back to his cell, de Champ sat and stared out the window of his study. He still didn't know what to think of his prisoner. Either the man was a stark raving madman, or he had watched too many American cowboy movies as a young boy. Either way, though, the cavalry was not going to come over the hill at the last moment and save him this time.

Something else still bothered him about Reese, however. From what de Champ had heard in the recording of the American's private conversations with the Winthrop woman, Reese appeared to be resigned to his fate. But just now he had acted totally unafraid, almost boastful, and it was difficult to know which was his true mental attitude. His empty threat to kick Clifford's ass if he was not exchanged immediately was pure bravado. But maybe he was just trying to bluff and not show fear in the face of the enemy.

That was an attitude that de Champ could understand, but it was not going to save either Reese or the woman. As soon as the Americans gave his brother back to him, both of his prisoners would have to die. They had seen his face and they knew where he operated from. They could never be allowed to go free now.

The Frenchman got to his feet and started for the radio room. It was time for his people in Saigon to make contact with Clifford to set up the exchange. If what Reese had said was true, he wanted to get his brother back while there was still something left of him. Damn the CIA!

SANTELLI WAS UP on point with Chief beside him scanning the open ground to their front. The terrain in this part of Cambodia was more open than the thickly jungled hills he was used to operating in, and he needed the sniper's long-range scope to help him look for the bad guys. So far, they had not made good time. The need for absolute security was forcing them to move extremely cautiously across the cleared ground, and they had had to hide several times to let roving NVA units pass them by.

"It's clear," Chief said, bringing the scope down from his eye.

Santelli motioned with his hand, and the two Nungs slipped out of their concealed positions and started across the open field bordering the rubber plantation. Once across, they took up positions under the trees and waved the rest of the team forward. One by one the men dashed across the open and ducked under cover.

Once the entire team was inside the rubber, they moved in an open, extended formation slipping from tree trunk to tree trunk. Santelli hated to move through rubber plantations, but there was no way to get around it this time. The whole place was one big rubber plantation, and you could see a man coming for a thousand meters through the open lanes between the ranks of trees. The only good thing about it was that if anyone was waiting for them, they had perfect fields of fire and observation, as well.

Ninh was on point with Santelli walking slack for him when the Nung frantically signaled for them to go to ground. Santelli dropped down and low-crawled up to the Nung's position. Peering around the side of a rubber tree trunk, he saw at least a platoon of North Vietnamese infantry sitting on the ground apparently taking a late lunch break. The men were clustered around a small fire heating ration cans, smoking and talking quietly among themselves.

The NVA were camped in a slight dip in the ground, and Ninh had walked right up on them without seeing them. Not knowing if they were part of a larger unit, Santelli motioned Kowalski up to his position to see if he could overhear any of their conversation.

The sergeant wiggled up on his belly and settled down beside Santelli to listen. "Oh shit!" he whispered. "Look over to your right, about twelve hundred meters out."

Santelli snapped his head around and, to his horror, saw a single NVA walking down the clear lane between the rubber trees heading directly toward their position. His head was down, and he was plodding along as though he didn't have a care in the world. Bringing his field glasses up to his eyes, the lieutenant saw that the man was carrying a message pouch over his shoulder. He was an NVA courier taking a short-cut through the shade of the trees.

The NVA platoon hadn't seen the courier yet, since the rise in the ground covered him from their sight. But unless the man deviated from his path, he was going to walk right into the Americans in just a few minutes.

Caught between the North Vietnamese platoon and the courier, the team couldn't pull back without a serious risk of being spotted. Santelli usually carried a silenced .22-caliber Ruger Mk-1 pistol with a telescopic sight in his ruck for occasions like this, but he had not brought it with him from Dak Sang. This time the sniper was going to have to take him out, but that presented a problem.

The Ruger was so effective for close-in silent kills because the .22-caliber round it fired was subsonic. After the pistol's silencer soaked up the noise of the muzzle blast, the round continued on its way completely silently because it did not break the sound barrier and did not create a sonic boom when the bullet left the pistol's muzzle.

The 7.62 mm round that Chief's M-14 NM fired, however, was supersonic. The silencer on the muzzle of the sniper rifle was not a true silencer; it was only a sound suppressor. The round broke supersonic when it came out of the end of the silencer and created a small sonic boom that could be heard for a hundred meters or so. The enemy platoon having lunch was only a little over a hundred meters away from them. It was risky, but he had to take the chance.

Santelli low-crawled over to the left flank where Chief and Cowboy were keeping an eye on the NVA. "Chief," he whispered. "We've got us a little problem. There's a Dink courier coming up on our right flank, and you've got to take him out."

The Indian frowned. "It's a big problem, LT," he whispered. "This rifle isn't completely silent—you can hear it when I fire."

"How loud is it?"

Chief shrugged. "Loud enough, I'm afraid." From where they lay, the wind brought them snatches of Vietnamese words as the NVA talked while they ate.

"We've got to take that guy out."

Chief looked thoughtful. "The wind is with us, and I will be firing away from them so maybe they won't hear it. Can you get me a poncho liner?"

"Why?"

"I'll fold it up and tie it over the end of the silencer to try to trap some of the sonic boom."

"You think it'll work?" Santelli asked.

"It can't hurt."

Santelli dug into the bottom of his ruck and got out his camouflaged poncho liner. The nylon quilt's filler was an open-weave synthetic material, and the dead air trapped in it should help muzzle the noise. Chief quickly folded the poncho liner into a half-metersquare and tied it around the end of the bulky silencer with one of his boot laces. He threw the rifle up to his shoulder to check that the blanket was not in the way of the line of sight of his scope.

"Let's try it."

Crawling on their bellies, the two men made their way around to the right flank. Snuggling up behind a tree, Santelli pointed out the courier, and Chief nodded. The sniper carefully focused the scope on the NVA's head. The only chance was for him to put a bullet into the man's brain. Under more normal circumstances, a bullet in the torso would do just as well, but this time the target had to go down without a sound. A yelp of pain, a scream or a gurgle might be overheard, so the only way to prevent that was to turn that guy's power off at the master switch, explode his brain.

Lining the cross hairs up on the bridge of the nose, he held his breath and took up the slack on the trigger. The rifle fired with a barely audible pop, and the NVA's head snapped back. The man crumpled to his knees like a puppet with the strings cut, and then went over onto his face into the red earth.

After ensuring that his target was down for good, Chief swung the rifle around in the direction of the enemy platoon. If the muffled shot had been heard, he had to be ready. The trick with the poncho liner seemed to have worked, though, as there was no sign of alarm from the platoon and he slowly relaxed.

A half an hour later the North Vietnamese started getting back into their rucks and grabbing their weapons to continue their march. Santelli gave them a full fifteen minutes to get out of the area before he got to his feet. This near-encounter had cost them valuable time, and they would have to move faster if they were to reach their jump-off point before the sun went down.

"Let's go," he growled.

REESE AWOKE from his nap when the guard brought their dinner. Even though she was hungry, when Laura saw Reese digging into the bowl of cold, sticky rice and small cut-up pieces of boiled chicken, skin and all, she pushed her bowl away.

Reese looked up from stuffing rice into his mouth with the first three fingers and thumb of his right hand. "You'd better eat that," he said.

She shook her head. "I'm not hungry."

"I didn't ask you if you were hungry, goddamn it," he snapped. "Eat it anyway."

"Okay," she snapped back. "I will, but please stop yelling at me."

Reese went back to his meal, and Laura's head dropped, silent tears forming in the corners of her eyes. Like the captive princess in the fairy tales, her hero had come to save her. But instead of comforting her, all he could do was yell at her and treat her like a child.

"Laura," he said, his voice a little less cold, "you've got to eat so you can keep up your strength. You're not going to be of any use to yourself or anyone else if you're weak from hunger."

"What are we going to do, Mike?" she allowed herself to ask.

"I don't know," Reese answered, his voice expressionless. "We're just going to have to wait and see. But you have to eat no matter what happens."

She took a pinch of the cold, gluey rice and put it into her mouth. It was almost tasteless, but she started salivating when it touched her tongue, and she reached for another bite. Before she knew it, the bowl was empty and she was still hungry. Reese had also finished his meal and was staring at the floor, his empty bowl beside him.

"Mike?"

He looked up. "Yes?"

"I'm sorry."

"About what?"

"About everything," she said. "I'm sorry I went through your briefcase that night, and I'm sorry you gave yourself up for me."

Reese shrugged. "It's just one of those things," he said. "We'll get it sorted out later."

"I really am sorry," she said. "I wish I could make you believe me."

"I know you're sorry," he answered. "But that doesn't count for much right now, does it?"

There was nothing she could say in answer to that.

DE CHAMP SMILED as he listened to the spiritless conversation between his two captives. From everything he was hearing, the fight seemed to have gone out of Reese. The Frenchman had expected a little more from a Special Forces officer, but in a way he was not surprised. From everything he had learned about the

Yankees over the years, they were a force to be reckoned with as long as they were winning, but they didn't have the internal strength to stand up under adverse conditions. Put them under pressure, and they folded quickly. Like their clown President Johnson, Reese had also proven to be a paper tiger, as the Chinese would say.

The Frenchman smiled. When he talked to the American again in the morning, he would increase the pressure on him. Before he set up the exchange for his brother, he wanted to have every last bit of information he could wring from Reese. Even though he had been forced to reveal himself to save his brother, he felt that there was still a chance he could continue his Saigon operation after he got Tran back. It was true that he would have to relocate his brother to a safe haven in Cambodia and would not have that avenue of information anymore, but maybe there was still something he could salvage from the wreckage.

It was worth a try at least. But to do that, he needed to know exactly how much the CIA knew about his operations in South Vietnam. The questioning would be rough on Reese, but the man was expendable.

It was too bad that Reese was not being more protective of the girl. If he were, it might be very profitable to threaten to work on her in order to get him to talk. That usually worked well when you had a man's woman in custody. But Reese had shown himself to be such a coward that it would probably be a waste of time that would be better spent by working on him more directly.

He would find out in the morning, though, after Reese had had a little more time in the cell. In his experience, there was little use in questioning a man until he had spent a day or two as a captive. Being a prisoner sapped a man's will very effectively. Particularly when the man was trying to make a brave show.

SANTELLI SLOWLY SEARCHED the area around the villa with the day scope from Chief's sniper rifle. After the brush with the NVA in the rubber, the team had been able to make better time, and they had reached their assembly area before dark. Lying beside him, Sergeant Kowalski used the lieutenant's field glasses and did the same. The sun was going down, and their observation position on the knoll overlooking the valley below gave them a clear view of de Champ's villa.

"This one's going to be real tough, LT," Kowalski said. "I've counted at least a dozen Dinks down there so far, and there's crew-served weapons on all four corners of the wall. They're all wearing black, but they look like NVA regulars to me."

Santelli took the rifle scope down from his eye. "Yeah, you've got that shit right," he said. "We're going to have to get real lucky to pull this one off."

"I still can't believe the captain would do something this stupid," Kowalski said in disgust. "Fucking women."

"I know."

"If he wasn't down there," Kowalski continued, "we could just call an Arc Light strike in on that place and blow it all to hell."

Santelli didn't bother pointing out that this was one of the main reasons why Reese had turned himself over to the Frenchman. Clifford would not have had even a second thought about having the entire Air Force drop bombs on Laura had she been there alone. But the CIA man knew that if he bombed the villa while Reese was in it, Santelli would hunt him down and kill him.

Santelli made a few more quick notations to the sketch of the compound he had drawn on the back of his map and put the sniper scope back in its case. "Let's go."

17

August 19, Mimot, Cambodia

Back at the assembly area, the rest of the team were preparing for the night assault when Santelli and Kowalski rejoined them. Black-and-dark-green camouflage paint had been applied to their faces and other exposed skin to cover every last inch. Camouflage paint was even more critical in close-quarters night operations because light reflecting off a sheen of sweat or skin oil could give them away.

They would leave their rucks behind in the assembly area, so they had loaded all the ammunition and grenades that they could carry on their assault harnesses. The only nonlethal items they carried were Silk Wilson's aid bag and their individual field dressings.

While the rest of the men tied their equipment down to make sure it wouldn't jingle or clank, the two Nungs put an extrasharp edge on their K-Bar fighting knives. Like most of the Chinese CIDG troops, these two were edged-weapons specialists. They would far rather slit a man's throat than merely shoot him, and tonight they would get a chance to do just that.

While Kowalski went to get his gear ready, the first thing Santelli did was to get on the radio to report back to Clifford. Since they were well out of the range of normal radio communication to Saigon with a PRC-77 radio, Santelli had to retransmit through the SOG long-range communications site on the top of Nui Ba Dinh Mountain north of Tay Ninh City. And even to do that, he had to rig a ground plane antenna to extend the transmission range of the small tactical radio.

Taking out his compass and a small roll of WD-1 commo wire, Santelli laid the premeasured length of wire on the ground in the exact compass azimuth for Nui Ba Dinh. The length of the antenna wire needed had been determined by the frequency the radio was set on. Stripping the installation from the end of the wire, he plugged it into the auxiliary antenna connection on the top of the radio.

After checking to make sure that the radio was set on the proper frequency, he keyed the handset. ''Bent Talon, Bent Talon, this is Bat Man,'' he radioed to the commo center on the mountaintop. ''Request retrans to Stone Tower on this push. Over.''

''Bat Man, this is Bent Talon,'' the retrans operator answered. ''Wilco, wait one, out.''

''Bat Man, this is Bent Talon,'' he came back a few seconds later. ''Go ahead with retrans to Stone Tower.''

''Stone Tower, Stone Tower, this is Bat Man, over.'' Santelli radioed.

''This is Stone Tower,'' Clifford answered immediately. ''Go ahead.''

''This is Bat Man,'' Santelli reported. ''We are in position to make the assault on the villa. We kept an eye on it for over an hour and we didn't see where they are being held, but I think they're inside. The moon won't be up until right after midnight, so we'll hit them at about 2300. Alert the chopper that we'll probably be calling him tonight for a pickup at Papa Zulu One. Over."

"Stone Tower, good copy. Your ride is spotted at Tay Ninh City and waiting your call on this push. Contact Red Dog. How copy, over?"

"Bat Man," Santelli replied. "Good copy. Negative further, out."

After working out a plan, Santelli called the team together for a final briefing. "I just checked in with Clifford, and our ride's waiting for us at Tay Ninh. As soon as we get this wrapped up tonight, we can go home.

"Here's the layout on the target," he said, showing them the sketch he had made on the back of his map. "There's several outbuildings on the grounds around the villa, but we didn't see anything that indicated any of them was being used as a prison. That means the Captain's probably being held inside the villa itself."

None of the men commented on the fact that Santelli didn't mention anything about looking for Laura if she wasn't in the same place Reese was. As far as they were concerned, their mission was to get their captain out of there and kill the Frenchman if they could. If they could free Laura in the process, so much the better. If they couldn't, tough shit, their job was to rescue their commander.

"Therefore, we're going to have to take the villa and here's how we're going to do it." He looked over at the sniper. "Chief, this is where you're going to earn your combat pay."

The Indian smiled.

"Here's what I want you to do."

LAURA STARTED AWAKE when she felt a rough hand clamp over her mouth. "Shh!" Reese hissed in her ear. "Listen, but don't say a word."

She relaxed and nodded her head.

"I want you to wake up now," he whispered, his mouth touching her ear. "We're going to have to move fast, and I need you to be alert."

She started to say something, but his hand clamped back tightly over her mouth. "Keep your mouth shut!" he hissed. "This is no time to be asking any of your dumb-ass questions!"

As he whispered to her, she could smell the strong scent of his sweat, and it brought memories rushing to her mind. The night he had made love to her in his bunker at Dak Sang, he had smelled that way—strong and powerfully masculine. Tonight, though, he was obviously not planning on making love to her. She didn't know what he was going to do, but she had a feeling that she wasn't going to like it.

"Put your shoes on and be ready to follow my orders," he whispered curtly. "I don't have time to argue with you right now or explain things to you. Your only chance to get out of this alive is to do exactly what I tell you to do when I tell you to do it. You got that?''

She nodded her head.

"Good. Put your shoes on and stand by. When I tell you to, start banging on the door and yelling for the guard. When he comes, I want you to use the word *Bac Si*. Tell him you want a *Bac Si*. You got that?''

She automatically started to ask him why he wanted her to do that, but nodded and kept her mouth shut.

Reese reached down and quickly unlaced his jungle boots. It would have been idiotic for him to try to smuggle a weapon in with him so he hadn't even tried. No one, though, seemed to have considered his boot laces to be a dangerous weapon, so he still had them to use as a garrote.

After tying the laces together to make a big loop, he tapped Laura on the shoulder and made twisting motions with his hand and pointed to the unlit, bare light bulb in the fixture on the ceiling. When she nodded that she understood what he wanted her to do, he cupped his hands and gave her a foot lift up to reach it. When she stepped back down and handed him the hot light bulb, he put it out of the way against the side of the wall.

Rolling up his blanket, he laid it on the cot and placed her blanket over it. In the light it wouldn't look like anything other than a rolled-up blanket, but in the dark it would do to draw the guard's attention to it for the few critical seconds he would need to take him out.

"Okay," he whispered, "start calling for the guard and remember to use the word *Bac Si*.''

CHIEF SLOWLY ADJUSTED the rear sight reticle of his
Starlight scope to focus it on the guard in the machine-gun bunker of the southwest corner of the
compound wall five hundred meters in front of him.
His firing position on the side of the hill allowed him
to cover the wall surrounding the compound, the villa
and most of the grounds. Only the area masked by the
wall in front of him and the villa itself was dead
ground for his rifle.

Though the moon was not out yet, the Vietnamese
manning the gun was plainly visible in the ghostly
green glow of the light-intensifying night scope. As
soon as the Indian sniper ranged in on him, he shifted
his sight picture down to the approach to the wall to
see if the assault team was in place. The glowing green
picture through the Starlight showed him the shad-
owed forms of six men crouching in the brush a few
meters from the wall.

Time to go to work.

Training his weapon back in on the guard, Chief got
a good sight picture again, held his breath and took up
the slack on the trigger. The rifle spit, and the guard
slumped forward over the edge of the sandbagged
emplacement. The sniper thought he saw the NVA
move and put another bullet into him for good mea-
sure before shifting his sight back to the men waiting
to go over the wall. As he watched, Santelli's team
raced across the open ground to the base of the low
wall. Once they were under cover again, the sniper
went back to scanning the area for trouble.

At the base of the wall, Hotchkiss and Kowalski braced their backs against the masonry and held their cupped hands out in front of them. Santelli put his boot in Ski's hands and climbed up on him like a ladder. Getting a firm grip on the top of the wall, he swung his leg up and over. To his right, Cowboy did the same. Lying motionless for a moment, he surveyed the compound.

Seeing that no one had noticed the guard take a round in the throat, he pulled his Randall fighting knife from the upside-down sheath taped to his assault harness and dropped on down inside. Landing softly, he crouched beside the base of the wall and motioned Cowboy down to join him. The Nung jumped down silently beside him, a broad-bladed K-Bar fighting knife in one hand and his Swedish K submachine gun in the other.

The compound was quiet; no one moved. The villa was blacked out, but beams of light showed around the edges of the curtains over the windows, and they could hear the faint sounds of Oriental music over the muffled chug-chug-chugging of a diesel-powered generator.

Taking a small rock from his pocket, he tossed it back over the wall in the prearranged signal for the rest of the team to join him. One at a time they silently scaled the wall and dropped down inside the compound. Once they were on the ground, they fanned out in a small semicircle, their fingers on their triggers.

REESE KEPT the garrote tight as he eased the guard's body to the floor. Summoned by Laura's banging, the man had not even been suspicious that the light had not gone on in the room when he'd flipped the switch. He had seen Laura pointing to the bundled form lying on the cot and had stepped right up to it. With the light out, the room had been in shadow, and Reese had been hiding in the dark with his boot lace garrote ready.

With a snap of his hands, Reese had thrown the boot laces over the guard's head and around his neck. Crossing his wrists, Reese had braced his knee against the small of the guard's back and pulled the garrote deep into the flesh of the neck. The VC had dropped his AK as his hands flew up to his neck, but he hadn't been able to get his fingers under the boot laces. His bladder released, filling the cell with the hot stink of urine, and his feet kicked a few times before he went limp.

Keeping the garrote tight, Reese checked the VC's carotid artery to make sure he was dead before releasing the laces from his neck. He glanced up and, in the dim light from the hallway, he saw Laura standing in wide-eyed shock, her fist jammed in her mouth to keep herself from screaming.

Ignoring her, Reese quickly stripped the guard of his Red-Chinese-style chest-pack magazine carrier and slung it around his neck. He would have liked to have had a couple of grenades, even the erratically fused Red Chinese stick-bomb versions, but the guard hadn't needed grenades for guarding prisoners inside the villa. He didn't have a knife, either, and his AK was one of the earlier types, which didn't have a folding bayonet under the barrel.

Picking up the assault rifle, he cracked the bolt open to make sure that there was a round in the chamber. He could see the base of a cartridge and, easing the bolt forward to lock again, he switched the selector switch on the side of the receiver down to semiautomatic fire. Slipping over to the open door, he listened carefully for any indication that his killing of the guard had been overheard, but there were only the normal sounds of a house at night.

Reaching for Laura's hand, he drew her to him. "Time to go."

OUT IN THE COMPOUND, Santelli and his men moved like shadows in the night as they checked the outbuildings one by one. So far, though, they had dry holed. They had slipped up on two of the guards and had silently slit their throats, but there had been no signs of Laura and Reese. If the captives were not being held in the last building, they were going to have to try to take the villa itself.

Using hand signals, Santelli motioned Kowalski and one of the Nungs forward. Their next objective was a long low building that looked as though it had originally been a horse barn and was probably used as a garage now. It was an unlikely prison, but it had to be checked anyway.

The sudden stuttering of an AK-47 on automatic fire broke the night's stillness. Santelli and his men went flat on their faces, their weapons up and ready. They didn't know who was firing, but it really didn't matter. Now that the villa was alerted, their element of surprise was lost.

"Pull back!" Santelli yelled.

REESE HELD Laura's arm in his left hand and the guard's AK in his right as he pressed his back against the side of the villa. The shit had just hit the fan and it looked as though they had stepped right in the middle of it.

At his feet lay the body of the VC who had suddenly come upon them out of the darkness. Reese had been a little slow bringing up the butt of his AK to smash his head in, and the man had reflexively triggered off a short burst before he died.

Reese had hoped to slip away from the villa silently, but that hope had vanished when the VC ran into them. They had made it up the stairs and out the back door without being seen. It had been purely a matter of a few seconds that Reese's eyes hadn't yet adjusted to the dark, and he hadn't seen the guard walking toward him in the deep shadows.

The short burst of fire had turned into a full-fledged firefight and, from the other side of the compound, he could hear the distinctive chatter of a CAR-15 on full-auto, punctuated by the flat crump of U.S. grenades. Obviously Santelli was out there, trying to rescue him. It was only bad luck that he had chosen to assault the villa at this particular time. Without a radio, though, there was no way that Reese could contact the lieutenant and let him know they had escaped. All they could do now was to run while they still had the chance.

The firefight, while a good diversion, would make it only that much more difficult for them to get away unseen. Men were running all over the compound, and the bright fingers of tracer fire crisscrossed the grounds. He would have liked to wait for things to calm down again before making his break, but he knew that if he did, someone would check the cell and find the guard's corpse. They had to be well clear of the villa before that happened.

He took Laura's arm again and said, "We have to make a break for it."

18

August 19, Mimot, Cambodia

From his position on the knoll, Chief watched the assault team race back across the compound for the safety of the wall. A door in the rear of the villa crashed open, and the bright rectangle of light disgorged half a dozen armed figures onto the grounds. The glare of white light from the open door rendered Chief's Starlight scope useless, and he jerked the rifle muzzle away so he would not burn out the scope's sensitive optics.

When the figures were clear of the bright light, the sniper brought them under his scope again. The reflected light from the door made the figures glow too brightly for him to make out any details. But when one of them stopped and fired toward the wall, he knew they were the enemy, not Santelli's assault team.

Sighting in on the lead man, he squeezed off a round and saw him go down. Shifting his sight, he fired again. It was up to him to give the men the covering fire they needed to make it back over the wall. The flash of a grenade explosion blinded him for a moment. Blinking his eyes, he went back to the scope to find another target.

1. How do you rate: _____

(Please print book TITLE)

1.6 ☐ Excellent   .4 ☐ Good   .2 ☐ Not so good
.5 ☐ Very good   .3 ☐ Fair   .1 ☐ Poor

GE 12345678

2. How likely are you to purchase another book:

In this *series*?

2.1 ☐ Definitely would purchase
.2 ☐ Probably would purchase
.3 ☐ Probably would not purchase
.4 ☐ Definitely would not purchase

By this *author*?

3.1 ☐ Definitely would purchase
.2 ☐ Probably would purchase
.3 ☐ Probably would not purchase
.4 ☐ Definitely would not purchase

3. How does this book compare with the action books you usually read?

4.1 ☐ Far better than others   .4 ☐ Not as good
.2 ☐ Better than others   .5 ☐ Definitely not as good
.3 ☐ About the same

4. What most prompted you to buy this book?

5. ☐ Read other books in series   8. ☐ Title   11. ☐ Story outline on back
6. ☐ In-store display   9. ☐ Author   12. ☐ Ad inside other book
7. ☐ Cover illustration   10. ☐ Advertising   13. ☐ Friend's recommendation

5. Which of the following other Gold Eagle action series have you read?

14. ☐ Executioner/Mack Bolan   20. ☐ Horn   25. ☐ Barrabas/SOBs
15. ☐ Stony Man   21. ☐ Time Warriors   26. ☐ Hatchet
16. ☐ Agents   22. ☐ Phoenix Force   27. ☐ Code Zero
17. ☐ Soldiers of War   23. ☐ Able Team   28. ☐ Time Raider
18. ☐ Survival 2000   24. ☐ Vietnam: Ground Zero   29. ☐ Cade
19. ☐ Deathlands

6. Which of the following categories of action fiction would you like to see more new series from or about?

30. ☐ Urban crime wars   37. ☐ Future crime wars   43. ☐ WW II combat
31. ☐ Anti-drug wars   38. ☐ Post-holocaust   44. ☐ Vietnam combat
32. ☐ Espionage   39. ☐ Future war   45. ☐ Paramilitary
33. ☐ Western   40. ☐ Anti-terrorist   46. ☐ Future techno-thriller
34. ☐ Science fiction   41. ☐ Martial arts   47. ☐ High adventure
35. ☐ Horror/occult   42. ☐ High-tech crime   48. ☐ Police drama
36. ☐ Other: _____

7. Where did you obtain this book?

49. ☐ Bookstore   53. ☐ Department/ discount store   55. ☐ Borrowed
50. ☐ Drugstore   54. ☐ Convenience store   56. ☐ Used
51. ☐ Supermarket   57. ☐ Other: _____
52. ☐ Military store

8. Please indicate how many action fiction paperbacks you buy in a month?

58.1 ☐ 1 or 2   .2 ☐ 3 or 4   .3 ☐ 5 to 10   .4 ☐ More than 10

9. Please indicate your sex and age group:

59.1 ☐ Male   60.1 ☐ Under 18   .3 ☐ 25 to 34   .5 ☐ 50 to 64
.2 ☐ Female   .2 ☐ 18 to 24   .4 ☐ 35 to 49   .6 ☐ 65 or older

Gold Eagle thanks you for sharing your opinions and returning this survey!

(61-65) ☐☐☐☐☐

Printed in Canada

NAME _____
(Please Print)

ADDRESS _____

CITY _____

ZIP CODE _____

BUSINESS REPLY MAIL

FIRST CLASS   PERMIT NO. 717   BUFFALO, NY

POSTAGE WILL BE PAID BY ADDRESSEE

NATIONAL READER SURVEYS

P.O. Box 1395
Buffalo, N.Y. 14240-9961

NO POSTAGE
NECESSARY
IF MAILED
IN THE
UNITED STATES

WHILE THE FIREFIGHT raged behind him, Reese kept to the darkness as he slipped around the side of the villa and headed for the front of the house. Since the fighting seemed to be concentrated at the rear of the compound, he was counting on the likelihood that guards usually stationed there had been drawn into the battle.

Peering around the corner of the house, he saw that the front grounds appeared to be empty. "Here's where we're gonna make a run for it," he whispered to Laura. "Head for the gate."

Taking her hand, he dashed out into the open. No shots rang out, and they covered the open ground in record time. Crouching in front of the wrought-iron gate, he gave Laura a boost up and she quickly climbed over the gate. As soon as she was clear, he scrambled up himself and dropped down on the other side.

Not wasting a second, he took her hand, and the two of them disappeared into the brush alongside the dirt road. Keeping to the brush, he ran until they reached the edge of the first stand of rubber trees. Ducking under the trees, he stopped for a moment so they could both catch their breath. He had absolutely no idea where Santelli planned to pull back to, but from what little he had been able to see of the surrounding terrain when he had arrived, he knew that it had to be somewhere on the high ground to the east of the villa. That was the only place where Santelli could hole up and still keep an eye on the place.

He would head east and hope that they could find their camp in the morning before the VC found them. "You ready to go?" he asked Laura.

She was still trying to catch her breath, so she nodded, her eyes big and frightened in the dark.

"Just keep close to me, and if we get into trouble, dive for cover."

DE CHAMP TOOK THE STEPS going down into the basement two at a time. Now that the firefight outside had stopped, he could check on his two prisoners. In the dim light of the hall leading to the cell, he saw that the door was still closed, but that didn't mean anything.

When he flicked on the light switch outside the door and the light did not turn on in the cell, he knew something was wrong. He opened the door, saw the body of the guard on the floor and knew all that he needed to know. The commando raid had been launched to recapture Reese and the woman. Now that they were freed and he had lost his bargaining chips, his brother's life wasn't worth a sou.

He spun around and raced for the radio room in the back of the villa. There were five thousand North Vietnamese and Vietcong troops in the area around Mimot, and if he alerted them in time, there was no place the raiders could hide where they couldn't be found. Even if they had a helicopter coming in to pick them up, the North Vietnamese could blanket the area and shoot it down.

He didn't care if Reese was captured dead or alive. Either way would work just as well to get his brother back. The thing he couldn't have, however, was for the Americans to escape and get back to Saigon. That would doom Tran for sure, and he could not allow that to happen.

CHIEF SAT in the darkness and watched the approaches to the team's assembly area. After successfully pulling out of the villa compound, Santelli had withdrawn the team to their hiding place to wait for daybreak. As soon as it was light, they would try to go in again if the place wasn't swarming with Vietcong. For now, though, all they could do was hole up and hope that no one stumbled into them tonight.

As he swept the sniper scope past the stand of rubber trees in the low ground to his front, he caught a glimpse of movement through the shadows. It was a little past midnight, the moon had risen, and when he focused the Starlight scope, he plainly saw that the first figure was carrying an AK-47. The assault rifle's curved 30-round magazine showed up clearly. The second figure, however, did not seem to be packing a weapon. There was something funny about the second figure, so he squinted and fine-tuned the scope again.

Yes, he was sure of it! The second figure was a woman. He could barely make out the shape of her breasts through the scope, but they were there. The only woman he knew anything about in this region was that woman reporter Captain Reese had gone after.

Releasing the pressure on the trigger of his rifle, he backed out of his position and crawled over to where Santelli was trying to sleep.

"LT," he said, and shook Santelli awake. "I think I've got something. I spotted a woman with big tits, but she's with a guy packing an AK."

"Are you sure?"

"About the woman? Yes."

"Show me."

It took a minute or two before Chief could find them again. Whoever they were, they were making pretty good time through the rubber trees. "There they are," he said, handing the scope to Santelli. "About two fingers left of that open space right below us and moving to the east."

Santelli spotted them immediately. And, as Chief had said, one of them was a woman and she definitely wasn't an Asian, not by at least three bra-cup sizes. From what he remembered of Laura, there couldn't be two women in all of Cambodia with those kind of chest measurements.

"That's got to be them," he said. "Let's go."

Pulling his red-filtered flashlight from his assault harness, Santelli started down the hill with Chief close behind him. Even with the night scope, down on the level ground it was more difficult to see between the trees. "I can't spot them," the sniper whispered.

Santelli stepped out into the open and, aiming the flashlight back into the trees, started blinking the light on and off. If he had made a mistake and the people they had spotted were Vietcong, he was dead. But he kept on signaling, thinking that it had to be Reese and Laura.

Reese finally spotted the blinking red light. Pulling Laura into cover behind a tree, he raised his AK.

"Dai Uy?" came a voice from the darkness. "It's me—Jack."

Reese released the pressure on the AK's trigger and stepped out into the open. "It's okay," he told Laura. "We've found Santelli."

"YOU WANT ME to call for mission closure, Captain?" Santelli asked as soon as they returned to the team's night position. "The chopper's waiting on the pad for us at Tay Ninh City. All we have to do is give him a call. There's an LZ we can use about two klicks away."

Reese shook his head. "No, we're not done here yet. We're going down after the Frenchman tomorrow. I want that bastard dead."

"Aren't we a little light on the ground for that, sir?" Kowalski asked cautiously. So far, it had all been good clean fun, but as far as he was concerned, there was no point in pushing their luck.

Reese's face wore a tight smile. "You've got that shit right, Ski," he said. "But we're going to do it anyway. If you want out, I'll let you stay back with her."

"What are you going to do with her?" Santelli asked, not looking in the direction where Laura sat out of earshot eating a C-ration meal.

"I'm going to leave her in the woods and come back for her later."

Santelli was stunned. "Sir?"

"You heard me." Reese's voice was low and hard. "I'm not going to risk us any further by trying to take her along. She'd just get in our road, and I can't spare anyone to stay behind with her."

"I don't think . . ." Hotchkiss started to say.

"Then don't," Reese snapped. "What's the ration situation?" he asked Santelli.

"We came packed for five days," the LT answered, "and have four days left. But with you two eating, that'll cut us down to three."

"We can go on short rations if we have to," Reese said. "But I don't think this is going to take us that long."

"What do you mean?"

"Now that we've gotten away," Reese explained, "the Frenchman is going to expect us to haul ass as fast as we can, so that's exactly what we're not going to do. He'll have every Dink in this part of Cambodia beating the brush for us, and we'll be lucky to make it even halfway to your PZ. We're going to keep our heads down tonight, and then we're going to go back down there after him. He'll never be expecting us to do anything like that."

"Captain," Santelli said formally, "can I speak to you alone for a minute?"

Reese smiled thinly at Santelli's uncharacteristic formal use of his rank. Unlike Regular Army, Special Forces was very lax about titles and formalities, and the XO generally called him either *Dai Uy* or Mike. His lapse into formality could mean that he wouldn't like what the LT was going to say to him.

"Sure."

Drawing out of earshot of the rest of the team, Santelli faced Reese. "Are you all right, sir?"

"Never felt better, Jack, why?"

The XO hesitated for a moment. "Then why are we doing this, sir? You're free and you got Laura out with you, so why don't we just get the hell out of here while we still can?" He shook his head. "I don't understand, sir."

Reese didn't fully understand it himself. All he knew was that he couldn't leave Cambodia until the Frenchman was lying dead at his feet. Logical or not, he had to kill de Champ—and not just because Dick Clifford wanted him dead, either. De Champ had to die because he was the Frenchman and the Frenchman had killed too many Americans. If he wasn't stopped, he would continue killing as soon as he could.

"Listen, Jack," he said seriously. "I'm going to take this guy out and I'll tell you why. Forget all about Laura and me being captured—that was just a sideshow. For the start, the sole purpose of this operation was to find the Frenchman and put him out of business, but he's still alive. So while I still have a chance, I'm going back down there to get him. It's as simple as that."

Santelli said nothing for a moment. As far as he was concerned, there had been nothing simple about this operation from the very beginning. This was another one of Clifford's classic CIA screwups, and the only reason he and Reese were involved at all was because Reese had been on hand to keep Jan Snow from being assassinated. From there, though, things had quickly gotten out of hand, and now it bore no resemblance to any military operation he had ever heard of: the fiasco in the Straight Edge, the semilegal snatch of Tran, Laura's getting kidnapped, Reese's surrendering to the Dinks, and now this questionable expedition into Cambodia. If word of any of this ever came out, they'd be lucky to just get life sentences in Fort Leavenworth.

"Let me help you with this, *Dai Uy*," Santelli finally said. "Since we're here, I guess we might as well see it through to the end."

Reese caught the use of the familiar nickname and relaxed a little himself. "Jack, listen. We've got to take that guy out while we're here and have a chance to do it. He ordered the hit on those guys in that Saigon restaurant and he tried to kill Jan. He's been a bad actor for years, and it's time that he got his ticket punched. If you want out, it's okay. You can take Laura and the guys on back to Saigon. I'll stay here with Chief and the Nungs."

Santelli shook his head. "I can't let you do that alone, *Dai Uy*. I came to get your ass outta here, and I'm not leaving without you."

Reese clapped him on the shoulder. "Thanks, Jack, I need all the help I can get."

"You're sure not lying there."

"MIKE," Laura said, and there was a quaver in her usually husky voice. She was still in a light state of shock when he rejoined her. "What's going to happen now?"

"We're going to stash you in the woods for safekeeping, and then we're going back there to kill de Champ before he can go into hiding again. Now that we know where he is, I have to take him out."

Laura looked out into the dark trees and shivered. The order had said to "terminate with extreme prejudice," and it looked like those orders were still in effect. "Mike...I don't want to be left alone here while you go back down there."

Reese shrugged. "I don't have any other choice. You're of no help to us right now, and taking you with us might get you killed. I've got to leave you behind."

Laura thought fast. "Maybe I can help you. Maybe I can distract him and make him think that you've completely left the area."

"What are you talking about?"

"What if I went back down there and told him that I was abandoned in the woods while the rest of you escaped? Wouldn't that help?"

Reese thought for a moment. "It would be pretty dangerous for you," he said slowly. "De Champ's no fool."

"It's dangerous for me to wait somewhere for you to get back, too." Her fear of being left behind showed in her voice. "What if you get cut off and can't get back to get me? Then I'll be captured anyway."

Actually a similar ploy had also occurred to Reese, but he had not voiced it, thinking that she would never go along with it. "Okay," he said. "Let's give it a try."

Laura shivered.

"We'll work the details out in the morning, though. Right now I think we both need to get some sleep."

"Mike?"

"Yes."

"I'm sorry."

He reached out and touched her lightly on the arm. "I know you are. We'll talk about it when we get back to Saigon and this is all behind us."

Since there was little more to say, Reese borrowed a poncho liner from one of the men and helped Laura clear out a bare spot for her to sleep on the ground. Clearing a place for himself beside her, he lay down on the bare ground and was asleep in seconds.

Even though she was exhausted, it was quite some time before Laura could get to sleep. The memory of Reese's killing the guard back at the villa kept running through her mind. Particularly the muted gurgling sound he had made as the boot laces choked the life out of him. She thanked God that his back had been to the dim light from the open door and she had not been able to see his contorted face as he died.

Even though she was warm under the borrowed poncho liner, she shivered and rolled over again to try to get comfortable. She had never seen a man killed up close before, and she was afraid that she would see it over and over again in her mind for the rest of her life.

19

August 20, Mimot, Cambodia

Lucian de Champ walked the grounds of his villa at first light the next morning. The bodies of his dead guards had not been taken away yet, and he could see the path the raiders had taken by the location of the corpses. The first two bodies had had their throats cut. It was only later that they bore bullet wounds or showed the marks of grenade frag. From the number of bodies with entry wounds in the back, he also knew that many of them had been cut down by their own comrades in the confusion of the night battle.

The thing he could not determine was whether the raiders had left with his two prisoners. He could only assume that they had, because why else would they have raided his villa? But from what he had been able to piece together from the evidence, the assault had not been well coordinated.

From the testimony of the survivors and the empty cartridge cases he had found on the ground, it looked as though the American assault team had been by the garage when the fight started. But the Vietnamese who had been found behind the villa with his skull crushed, as well as the fact of the empty cell, indicated that someone had gotten close to the house. Maybe the fight had erupted on their way back out.

Just then, one of his guards came up to him. "Monsieur de Champ," the man said, "a long-nosed woman is coming down the road."

De Champ thought he was hallucinating when he turned and spotted the lone figure limping down the dirt road toward the villa. That long mane of blond hair and full figure could only belong to one woman in this part of Asia. Taking one of his guards with him, he started toward her.

"Laura!" he called out, waving the guard back when he got close enough to see that she wasn't armed. "What are you doing here?"

"They left me," she answered, not able to keep a choked-off sob from her voice or the tears out of her eyes. "Once Mike joined up with the rest of them, they just ran away and left me. They thought they heard some NVA in the woods, and they took off running. I couldn't keep up with them, and they didn't come back for me."

Laura definitely looked like someone who had been left behind. Her long hair was wildly tangled, her face was scratched, her clothes were dirty and the top two buttons of her blouse had been ripped off, revealing the firm roundness of her full breasts. She looked as though she had spent the past few hours running wildly through the woods.

The thought crossed de Champ's mind that maybe he had been a little hasty in condemning Laura to death. Since this recent turn of events was sure to cost him dearly, maybe he could recover some of the costs through her. It had been a long time since he had had a piece of merchandise quite as nice as this. Once she was cleaned up, she would bring a good price on the white-slave market. He knew several men who would pay dearly for a blonde with a face and body like hers. It would be too dangerous for her to be sold to anyone in Vietnam, but there was still the rest of Asia and the Middle East to consider.

"Come on in, my dear," he said taking her arm. "You can clean up inside, and I think I may have some clothes that will fit you."

"Could I have something to eat, too, please?" she said, tears forming in the corners of her blue eyes. "They said they couldn't stop long enough for me to eat."

Although de Champ hated white women, especially blondes who reminded him of his mother, something about Laura's vulnerability got through to him. He had known Reese to be a coward, but to his mind, this went further than mere cowardice. Even though he intended to turn Laura into an opium addict and sell her as a sex slave, he would never have treated a woman the way Reese had treated her.

Laura glanced out of the corner of her eye at de Champ. Reese had been right. It looked as though he had fallen for it hook, line and sinker. All she had to do now was to keep playing the role until Reese and Santelli could come to rescue her.

"WHAT DID OUR FAVORITE spook have to say?" Santelli asked as Reese handed the radio handset back to Cowboy.

Reese grinned. "In plain language, he said that I was out of my fucking mind. He also said that if I got Laura killed, he was going to see to it that I wound up in jail right alongside him."

"That's a bit of a switch, isn't it?" Santelli said. "He's the one who thought you were insane for coming to get her in the first place."

"That was before I got her out of there," Reese replied. "I think he was planning on taking the credit for having freed a female American citizen from the clutches of the infamous Frenchman. You know, Dick Clifford, boy hero of the CIA."

Santelli chuckled.

Reese glanced down at his watch. "She should be down there by now, so we'd better get going. I don't want to leave her there too long."

"Ready when you are, *Dai Uy.*"

DE CHAMP LED LAURA into one of the bedrooms on the main floor of the villa. "You can get cleaned up in there," he said, pointing to the bathroom. "And I will have something brought for you to wear."

After she locked the door behind her, Laura quickly poured a tub full of hot water. Although she would have liked to soak in it for hours, she quickly washed the grime of the past several days from her body and shampooed her hair. She was toweling her hair dry when a young Vietnamese woman walked in with her arms full of clothes. "Please," the girl said shyly. "These clothes for you."

"What is your name?" Laura asked as she took the clothes.

"My name Mei," the girl answered, casting her eyes to the floor so as not to stare at Laura's nakedness.

"Where do you live?"

"My home here, I belong Monsieur de Champ."

Laura didn't know what to say to that. Either the girl was de Champ's mistress or his slave. From what Reese had told her about the Frenchman's white-slave trading and his bordellos, she could be either one. Either way, however, she was not likely to be a potential ally.

She hurriedly dressed in the tan pants and white blouse the woman had brought and slipped back into her own shoes. When she had brushed out her still-damp hair, the Vietnamese girl led her into the dining room where a single meal had been laid out on the table.

REESE CROUCHED in the brush and watched the NVA patrol pass some hundred meters in front of him, heading out as fast as they could go. This was the fourth patrol they had seen so far during the morning, and it was not yet 1000 hours. De Champ must have notified every Vietcong in the neighborhood to be on the lookout for them. If he had not been able to convince Santelli to come along with him, and the team had tried to make a run for it, they would probably all be dead or captured by now. As it was, none of the troops searching for them were paying much attention to the areas close to the villa.

He slowly got to his feet and motioned the team forward. He had told the chopper pilot that they would be ready for pickup by 1200 hours, and if they were going to make it on time, they had to get a move on it.

IT WAS A LITTLE EARLY for lunch, but Laura did not have to feign hunger as she sat down to the meal waiting for her. The meals she had been fed in the cell had hardly been gourmet quality, and she had eaten little enough over the past two days. The coffee was strong, Continental style, the bread and fruit fresh and the cold roast pork delicious. It was easily the best meal she had had in weeks. She also had a sinking feeling that if Mike's plan didn't work, it could well be her last.

As soon as she had finished, de Champ led Laura into his study. "Now that you are refreshed," he said, giving her a charming smile, "maybe we can talk about your future."

She smiled back at him faintly. "I'm glad that I am going to have a future," she said. "Mike made me think that you were going to kill me."

"I think I have proven him wrong, Miss Winthrop." De Champ sounded sincere. "And, speaking of your Captain Reese, how many men did he have with him on this raid?"

Laura hesitated. This was not something she was prepared to talk about; Mike hadn't briefed her about anything like this. Should she tell him the truth, or should she lie? And, if she lied, how many men should she say she saw. "It was dark," she stalled. "And I couldn't see them clearly."

"But surely you can make an estimate," he prompted her. "Were there a dozen, two dozen?"

She thought fast. "Two dozen, I think. But like I said, it was dark and I couldn't see them."

De Champ sighed. "You are not telling me the truth, my dear. Not more than half a dozen men assaulted this compound last night. If he had had more troops with him, I am sure he would have used them."

His arm swung wide to take in the room's furnishings. "We can take this discussion to some place less comfortable if you like," he went on, his voice like a whip. "But I will have the truth out of you one way or the other. Your captain and his CIA comrades are still holding my brother captive, and I mean to get him released."

"I'm sorry," Laura said softly. "I'll tell you everything you want."

"I will free my brother," de Champ went on as if she had not spoken. "And if he has been hurt, they will pay dearly for his blood."

IT WAS COMING ON to high noon, and Reese and Santelli lay on the knoll overlooking the villa below. Chief was a few meters off to their right flank, peering through the day scope on his rifle. From what they could see, few people were stirring in the compound. The curtains were drawn back from the windows, but with the house in shade, he could see very little in the unlit rooms inside.

The good news was that the compound was almost unguarded. The crew-served weapons positions in the guard towers were empty, and only two men guarded the front gate. Fortunately the gate wasn't masked by the house, and Chief could easily take care of them.

He turned to the sniper. "Okay, you know what to do."

The Indian nodded.

"Let's get it," Reese said to the other men.

The six men got up from their positions and followed him down the knoll.

STILL TALKING about his brother, de Champ was walking toward Laura when he caught something out of the corner of his eye. The main window of his study looked out into the front yard of the compound and, when he turned, he saw that the two men who should have been standing guard on the gate were lying on the ground. From their crumpled postures, he knew that they were dead.

"Bitch!" de Champ's arm flashed out. Grabbing Laura's thick hair, he savagely twisted, jerking her closer to him. "You lied to me! They came back with you!"

Laura screamed and tried to pull away, but his grip on her hair could not be loosened.

Twisting her face around to him, he hammered his fist into the side of her head. Dazed by the blow, she slumped to her knees. Dragging her along the floor by her hair, he lunged for the alarm button on the wall behind his desk. Before he could reach it, he heard the sounds of gunfire on the grounds, followed by the hollow crump of a grenade.

Holding tightly to Laura, the Frenchman pulled open a desk drawer and grabbed the U.S.-issue .45-caliber pistol inside. Racking back the slide to chamber a round, he shoved her in front of him as a shield as he moved for the door. A burst of fire rang out from inside the house, and de Champ dropped back against the wall.

"Laura!" Reese called out from the end of the hall outside the study.

With the muzzle of the pistol pressed against the side of her head, Laura did not answer.

"De Champ!" Reese called out again. "If you let her go, you can live!"

The Frenchman's only answer was two quick shots from the .45 pistol that punched through the door.

There was no way that Reese could storm into the room without getting killed. He had to get de Champ out into the open. Snatching a grenade from his ammo pouch, he pulled the pin. Lofting the grenade like a softball, he tossed it as far as he could down the long hallway.

The explosion shook the villa, the frag spattering the walls. "The next one's in your face!" Reese shouted.

"Merde!"

Holding Laura in front of him, de Champ stepped out into the open doorway, his .45 blazing.

Ignoring the bullets singing past him, Reese took a good firing stance and triggered off two aimed rounds on semiautomatic. The first shot grazed the side of de Champ's shoulder, making him jerk to the side, and the second round went into the center of his chest.

The Frenchman slumped, his fingers loosening their grip on Laura's hair. She pulled free and staggered back as he fell to the floor.

Reese rushed into the room, the smoking AK in his hand. Ignoring Laura, he walked over to the fallen de Champ, took careful aim at the middle of his forehead and fired one shot. De Champ's body arched with the impact of the bullet before going completely limp.

The Frenchman was terminated.

REESE WAS CHANGING the magazine in his AK when Santelli burst into the room. "The house and grounds are cleared, *Dai Uy*," he reported. "And the chopper's in-bound. His ETA's in zero four."

"Good," Reese replied as he slung the weapon over his shoulder and reached down to help Laura to her feet. "Let's get out there and make sure the LZ's secure. Someone might have heard the firing."

"Mike," Laura said. "There's a Vietnamese woman somewhere around here, de Champ's mistress or something like that. Maybe we should take her with us."

Santelli shrugged. "We didn't see her."

"I don't care," Reese said. "Let her stay here. She's probably VC anyway."

"Look out, Mike!"

Reese spun around and saw a young Vietnamese woman standing in the doorway, the AK in her hands coming up to fire. Caught with his own weapon slung over his back, Reese fumbled to get to it.

Santelli's CAR-15 blazed in his hands, and the burst of 5.56 mm caught Mei across the chest. A look of surprise came over her eyes, and her mouth formed a small O. The AK fell from her nerveless fingers, and she slowly crumpled to the floor beside the body of de Champ.

As Mei's blood pooled on the floor, Laura heard the sound of helicopter rotors in the distance, approaching fast.

"Come on," Reese said urgently, grabbing her arm. "It couldn't be helped. We've got to go now."

Laura resisted him for a moment.

"Come on!"

She let Reese lead her away.

20

August 22, Tan Son Nhut

When Laura walked out of Clifford's second-floor office in the SOG headquarters building at Tan Son Nhut, she was completely exhausted, both physically and mentally. The events of the past several days had taken a heavy toll on her, and the lengthy SOG debriefing had been the final straw that had broken the back of her endurance.

Clifford had been brutally frank about what would happen to her if she were to write a single word about the Frenchman operation. He had not threatened and blustered like Colonel Marshall had done the first time she had tried to expose SOG's activities. He had simply told her the way it would be and had cited several government regulations she had never heard of to back up what he said. He then handed her a two-page document that reiterated what he had told her. She had read it over and then signed it to signify that she understood her responsibilities under the security and espionage regulations of the United States and was aware of the penalties that would be inflicted upon her should she violate them.

As she waited in the hall while Reese had a final word with the CIA agent, her head ached. She had not

realized how much power the government could bring
to bear on a citizen who crossed the sharp line between curiosity and espionage. Journalistic freedom
of the press didn't amount to much compared to what
she had just read.

The door opened and Reese stepped out. "I'll walk
you downstairs," he said.

Neither one of them spoke as they walked down the
hall and took the stairs leading to the ground floor. As
they approached the front door, Laura stopped. "Are
you coming by later tonight?"

When he turned to face her, his eyes were kind and
his voice gentle. "No, Laura, I'm not. I'm flying back
to Dak Sang this afternoon."

"Do you have to go today?"

"Yes, I do."

There was a finality in his voice that told her more
than his few words. "Why, Mike?"

"It just has to be that way."

"I don't understand."

"I know you don't," he said. "And there's something else you don't understand, as well, and it has to
do with what is going on over here."

Laura frowned. "What do you mean?"

"The war." Reese's arms opened to encompass the
entirety of Southeast Asia. "And what it really
means."

"I don't understand."

"I know you don't." There was a note of sadness in
his voice. "And I'm not sure that you ever will."

"Damn it," she said, a touch of anger creeping into her voice. "Quit talking around in circles. Tell me what you mean."

"It's simple," he said. "To people like you, the war is like a circus. It's exotic, exciting, entertaining and sometimes quite profitable."

"That's not fair," she said angrily.

"To some," he continued as if he had not heard her outburst, "it's a God-sent opportunity to make a fortune. Most of the Vietnamese black marketers have American contacts. To the politicians, both American and Vietnamese, it's their chance to seek power and enforce personal agendas. To some high-ranking officers, God rot their souls, this war is their long-sought opportunity to gain rank and fame through the blood of their troops. What you all have in common is that you're all vultures . . . and as long as the killing continues you will be well fed."

"What about you?" she said. "You're part of this war, too. You're feeding on it as much as we are."

His eyes held hers for a moment before he answered. "To me, and to those who think like me, this war is a tragedy on a major scale."

He held up a hand to stop her from automatically agreeing with him. "Not because of the killing and dying. Killing and dying we will always have with us, and that itself is not the problem. This war is a tragedy because in the long run all the killing and dying is going to be for nothing."

"What do you mean?"

"What I mean is that when the crowd has had its fill, the circus will be over, the crowd will go home and this country will be left behind. Nothing permanent will have been accomplished here because the people who should have cared about the war's outcome have cared only for their narrow, selfish interests. The dead will be quickly forgotten, and everyone will go on about their business."

For a moment Laura said nothing. While she did not agree with everything he had said, she was honest enough to recognize that there was truth to it. "What are you going to do now?" she finally asked.

Reese grinned. "Me? I'm going to stay here as long as I can. I have a lifetime contract to play my role in this drama, and I have to see it out to the end."

"What's going to happen to us?" Her voice was almost a whisper.

"There is no *us*," he said gently, his voice trying to soften the blow. "You have your agenda and I have mine. And as we have learned over the past week, they are not the same."

"But what am I going to do?"

"If you're smart, you'll go back to the States as soon as you can and forget that you were ever over here. Maybe you'll go on to bigger and better things in your profession, maybe you'll even get married and raise a house full of rug rats. Every now and then you might remember something from this time and smile. Maybe you'll even remember me occasionally." He smiled. "Hopefully with affection."

He hugged her, taking no note of the tears forming in her eyes. "Goodbye, Laura."

MIKE REESE STRAIGHTENED the green beret on his head as he stepped briskly out of the SOG building. Overhead, the sun blazed down, and he felt the sweat break out down the center of his back. By midafternoon it would be a scorcher, but by then he would be back in his mountaintop camp with his fist wrapped around a cold beer while he listened to Sergeant Pierce tell him what had happened during his absence. Later that evening he would go to the mess hall and eat dinner with the Nungs. Their crude jokes and laughter would be their way of telling him that they were glad to see him back.

Still later he would go to bed and, hopefully, sleep dreamlessly. Thoughts of Laura would not tease his mind. He would not waste time thinking about what he would do if he went back to the States and took up housekeeping with her. He would sleep soundly and wake in the morning, prepared to go out once more to face what had to be faced with a clear mind.

His old drill sergeant had said that if the Army had wanted him to have a wife, he would have been issued one, and that went double for girlfriends. He still had a war to fight, and as long as he wore the green beret, the war had to come first.

Dan Samson finds himself a deciding factor in the Civil War in the third thrilling episode of the action miniseries...

TIMERAIDER

John Barnes

Dan Samson, a hero for all time, is thrown into the past to fight on the battlefields of history.

In Book 3: UNION FIRES, the scene has switched to the Civil War, and Vietnam veteran Dan Samson works to free a leading member of the biggest resistance group in the South.

Available in December at your favorite retail outlet.

TAKE 'EM FREE

4 action-packed novels plus a mystery bonus

NO RISK
NO OBLIGATION TO BUY